- STEPHEN CL

THE COMEDOWN AND OTHER STORIES

- UNNA2URAL WAX -

STEPHEN CLARKE 1980

Northern Irish writer and electronic musician.

Based in Edinburgh, Scotland.

https://www.amazon.co.uk/-/e/B077VG4VKS

https://stephenclarke1980.bandcamp.com/

https://twitter.com/stephenclarke80

https://www.instagram.com/stephenclarke1980/

ALSO BY STEPHEN CLARKE 1980

DELETED SCENES: MY AUTOBIOGRAPHY (2017)

KEEP DREAMING: A GUIDE TO REAL LIFE (2018)

NO REST FOR THE LISTENER (2019)

AVAILABLE FROM AMAZON

AND ALL GOOD BOOK SHOPS

STEPHEN CLARKE 1980

THE COMEDOWN AND OTHER STORIES

- STEPHEN CLARKE 1980 -

THE COMEDOWN AND OTHER STORIES

THIS BOOK IS A WORK OF FICTION.
ANY RESEMBLANCE BETWEEN THESE FICTIONAL
CHARACTERS AND ACTUAL PERSONS,
LIVING OR DEAD, IS PURELY COINCIDENTAL.

ALL RIGHTS RESERVED.
NO PART OF THIS PUBLICATION MAY BE
REPRODUCED, STORED IN A RETRIEVAL SYSTEM,
OR TRANSMITTED, IN ANY FORM OR BY ANY
MEANS, WITHOUT THE PRIOR WRITTEN
PERMISSION OF THE COPYRIGHT HOLDER.

AN UNNA2URAL WAX PRODUCT.
MADE IN LOCHEND, EDINBURGH, SCOTLAND.

2023.

DEDICATION

For Bill Drummond and Nina Kraviz.

Thank you both for your help, support and kindness.

Keep dreaming,

Stephen x

EPIGRAPH

Clarke lives by his own rules,

has a distinct vision of how he wants

his art to be formed,

and is not one for compromise.

For me, these qualities define a real artist.

- Scaramanga Silk

TABLE OF CONTENTS

i. PREFACE

01. THE COMEDOWN

02. DEATH NOTES

03. LIGHTS OUT IN THE BOOTH

04. BEN SMYTH

05. FEAR OF FALLING

06. COVID SHEBEEN

07. THE PLANT ROOM

08. HOW I GOT MY SCAR

09. FREYA LOVES GRACE

10. THE LIGHT

#ii POSTFACE

iii. AFTERWORD BY SCARAMANGA SILK

iv. ACKNOWLEDGEMENTS

i. PREFACE

In late November 2019 I wrapped a kilt around my waist and boarded a train in Edinburgh destined for Liverpool. I was on my way to DJ for The JAMs at WAKE L8, an event I had devised to celebrate the lives of The MuMufied who were about to join The People's Pyramid. Nina Kraviz sent me a message to let me know that she was so proud of me, along with a link to a collection of unreleased material and every track that had ever been released on her label, TRIP. No Rest For The Listener, my latest book, had become a number one bestseller. Shortly before my train journey Bill Drummond had bought me a pint in Leith Theatre. That Summer I had met Bill at the premier of Best Before Death, where he handed me the first copy of his new book, White Saviour Complex. I had also travelled to Bill's Curfew Tower, where I met my favourite poet, Hollie McNish. Finally, after decades of creating and deleting work, I felt like I was living the life I had dreamed of. However, this feeling was soon quarantined due to a global pandemic.

I had been hailed as a hero by several people for the simple act of buying a large pack of loo roll during the Curfew Tower Curry Night. By the time the UK had went into lockdown my friend, Budgie, joked that my purchase had been a visionary act, as shoppers around the World scrambled to buy trolley loads of toilet paper. While working from home became commonplace and I found myself watching empty buses pass by my house each rush hour, I began to contemplate my next move. Scaramanga Silk contacted me to suggest I try writing fiction. He's one of the few people I listen to when it comes to creativity. So, I began to research how to construct a short story, amassed a small library of fiction titles by authors like James Kelman, Laura Hird and Bernard MacLaverty, and wrote my first tale, The Light. Whenever I turned 40 Bill Drummond warned me that it would be one of the more difficult years of my life, but that I'd get through it. As ever, he was right. I could feel that my mental health was breaking down and my, once prolific, artistic output slowed to a crawl. So, I began to write stories that tried to capture this loss of youth.

My process when writing this book involved sharing everything I created with an online audience. This mainly involved me uploading short video readings of the latest page I'd written but, occasionally, I would upload a block of text. These extracts were often simply the opening paragraph of a new story. Most of the time these were met with words of encouragement and intrigue from friends. That was until I uploaded the first passage of a new tale titled The Comedown. Within hours I had been contacted by ageing Ravers from America to Australia who were keen to read the rest of a story I hadn't yet written. Many of these people wanted to let me know that the opening of The Comedown chimed perfectly with what they had been thinking and feeling for several years. So, over the months that followed, I poured myself into that story. I had notes scrawled all over the place, I listened to the music that the characters listened to, and I did my very best to weave it all together with as much honesty as I could. Therefore, I've decided to make The Comedown the title story of this collection. I'll get back to you in the Postface. Enjoy the ride!

01. THE COMEDOWN

Most people seem to think that The Comedown was something that was dealt with over the course of a Manic Monday and a Suicide Tuesday back in the nineties. In reality, The Comedown is living long enough to see your dropping mate dressed in a suit and hearing them sound all hyped about an office party. Meeting old faces from Raves online before noticing that they blame all of their problems on foreigners and write things like "Take me back!" under old Prodigy videos. Screaming into an abyss about smartphones being used at Raves that they don't go to because it's no longer 1992. When I was a teenager there was a Teddy Boy who used to stand around street corners up the town. My mates would laugh and point at him because he stood out. He was probably old enough for a bus pass, wearing a drape jacket and brothel creepers with a shoestring tie and what was left of his hair slicked back. I was drawn to the guy though. He was kind of cool, representing his tribe. The last Ted in town.

There's always a reason why you feel drawn to things. It's usually because whatever it is that has caught your eye is mirroring something inside you. Like me paying attention to that Teddy Boy all those years ago and sort of understanding what he was up to. I could see in his eyes that he wasn't playing fancy dress. He was saying something without talking. That Ted was letting the town know that someone was still listening to Eddie Cochrane and thinking about breaking a few legs with an iron bar. I could feel that. The guy made an impression on me. I was talking about the Teddy Boy at a house party a few years ago and a lad there remembered him. He said that the Ted had fallen from a height when he was a teenager and there was something wrong with his brain after that. He was frozen in time with the mind he'd had before he fell. The Ted knew every last detail about the fifties but he couldn't tell you what he'd eaten for breakfast. That's what the lad at the party told me anyway. He said the Teddy Boy had lived with his Mum until she died, but he wasn't sure what had happened to him after that. We both reckoned he'd be dead by now.

My Granny would have been from the same generation as that Ted and there was probably something wrong with her brain too. She had two front rooms. Well, one of her front rooms was at the back of the house, but it was still a front room. The front room at the back of the house is the one we all used. The furniture was falling apart in there and the carpet was threadbare in the shape of a semicircle from the hall door to the entrance to the kitchen. The good front room at the front of the house was always kept immaculate. It had a large coffee table that my Granny polished every week and a long settee that was as good as new, because nobody had ever sat on it. That front room was kept for special occasions, like when my Grandad died. Granny gave the undertakers permission to use the good front room for his wake. I can remember looking through the window with the rest of my family and seeing Grandad in his coffin in the middle of the good room, with the large coffee table resting upside down on top of the unused settee behind him. Dad told me the last time Grandad had been in the good room he had painted the walls.

There is a theory that human behaviour can ripple through time. My Granny probably kept a good front room that no one could ever use because her Mum was an alcoholic who had turned to drink because her Dad had killed people during the First World War. That intergenerational stress may have built up inside my Granny to the point at which she felt the need to create a space she could control. That makes sense to me. Intergenerational trauma rippling through time may be why I'm sat here in one of my Vauxhall Nova SR 1.3's at five in the morning beside a supermarket that won't open until six. On the outside I hope everyone will see that I'm still as cool as ever. I want them to think I'm the same lad I was back when I Raved through the night in the field that was here before they built the supermarket. On the inside though, I'm really struggling. I've typed all of my feelings into a search bar on the internet to try and work out what I need to do to fix myself. I've been thinking of my broken brain like it's one of my motors. Hoping that someone will have posted a video tutorial detailing how to get me up and running again.

I can buy a lot of the trendy clothes from my youth online now. Some of the clobber is the real deal, vintage clothing they call it, but there are loads of fakes too. Brands like Joe Bloggs, Trip To Eclipse, Spliffy and No Fear. I've stopped wearing No Fear gear though, ever since my social anxiety started to become overwhelming. It wouldn't feel right sitting here in my Nova, in the dark, with my earplugs in, the windows rolled up, the sunroof wound down and all the other seats loaded up with black plastic bags filled with balloons, while I'm wearing clothes with No Fear printed on them.

I came up with the idea of filling the car with bags a few weeks ago, the morning after I'd driven up to the reservoir with Tina Short. I hadn't seen her in years. So, I took my other Nova out for a spin, the good one. It's a 1.3 SR like the one I'm sitting in now, but instead of being mustard yellow with grey wheel trims it's glacier white with 3 spoke alloys. That car turns heads, so I need to be in the right mood to go out in it. If I wake up in the morning and I'm not filled with a sense of dread or panic then I feel like I can go out in my good motor.

Tony was out of town on a team building exercise with his work when Tina dropped me a message saying she was bored. I sent her a link to a good stand up comedy video with this American guy doing impressions, but she asked if we could go for a spin because she wanted to get out of the house. It seemed a bit odd to me as I only really keep in touch with the pair of them online now. Tony used to be my dropping mate back in the day, but I got sick of watching him turning into his Dad. He actually got a job in the same accountancy firm as his Dad, dressed like his Dad and drove the same Volvo as his Dad, that's how bad it was. The last time I went to their place was at least 5 years ago. Tony was manning his new barbecue and pointing at his decking. Tina was going on about how they'd decided to spend more money on their house after she'd found out she couldn't have kids. I raced out of there. As soon as I'd eaten my burger I whispered to Tony that my stomach was playing up and I ran to my car. I laughed when I saw him in my wing mirror scratching his head and looking at his barbecue. That was funny.

I have a cupboard full of medication to help with my anxiety and depression. Although, I very rarely take it the way my doctor asks me to. Some days I'm in a good mood and I just don't bother with any pills. That can lead to a dip though, like a day when I just want to sleep because it's better than being awake. Once I get beyond that and I'm up and about then my mood can go the other way and I try to just stay awake. Bed becomes the enemy. I could be up for a few days in a row. I get very spaced out doing that though. Whenever I finally get to bed it can be difficult to go to sleep because my mind is still really alert, but my body is just limp and tired. Sometimes I wonder if my death is going to feel like that. I reckon I should have died when I was younger. I'm not suicidal, I just think that dying young is probably better than getting old, and not being born in the first place might be as good as it gets.

I swallowed a load of pills the night we went up to the reservoir. Most of them were prescribed to calm my thoughts and get me out of my front door and into the car. The other pills were ecstasy, courtesy of Tina.

Tony's house is a new build out in the suburbs. It took a while for me to drive out towards it. Tina text me to say she'd meet me outside the hairdressers near the Ring Road, even though I said I'd be happy to drive up to her house. Tina replied that she just fancied a stroll. It's not much of a walk if you ask me. Through their soulless neighbourhood, past the entrance to an industrial estate and up an embankment to a row of shops that were all shut for the night apart from an Indian takeaway. I had the radio on and they were playing Dance classics. Really cheesy tunes that I wouldn't be caught dead with in my record bag but some of them had me reaching over to turn the volume up. As soon as I drove onto the Ring Road they started playing God Is A DJ by Faithless. The Nova has a top speed of 101 miles per hour and the road was empty at that time of night. For a few minutes I felt really alive. I was wide awake and living in the moment. The music seemed to be in time with the street lights I was rushing past and I was tapping out the beats on my steering wheel. I can remember that I felt like closing my eyes forever.

Tina was resting with her back against the shutters of the hairdresser's with her arms crossed, like she was cold or annoyed. It was kind of funny to me because she was dressed a bit like a teenage Punk, and the last time I'd seen her she'd been wearing a long, floral, dress, flouncing around her garden looking like someone who taught elocution lessons. I have to admit she was actually looking pretty cool and her attitude matched her outfit. That sort of thing is very important, whether you're a Punk, a Mod, a Rocker, a Raver or even a Teddy Boy, you need to be in the zone and own the look. If you aren't in the mood then don't risk a full-on outfit. Just dress like Bruce Springsteen did for Born In The U.S.A., or like Kylie Minogue did back when she was on Neighbours. Plain t-shirts and blue jeans or dungarees. Workwear is your saviour when you want to be ignored. Tina was wearing black boots with red fishnet stockings, a red tartan kilted skirt, a tight black t-shirt with a red anarchy symbol, a light blue denim jacket that was ripped and frayed and there was a small, red, leather bag covered in metal studs resting against her right hip.

I bounced the Nova up onto the kerb, just a tiny bit, to get a reaction from Tina. Her face broke into a smile and she pretended to kick the front bumper as she walked around to the passenger door. I switched the radio off as she got in, just in case she thought I liked driving around the town listening to Paul Van Dyk. I wasn't prepared for the tidal wave of smells that washed over me as soon as she'd closed the door behind her. It was a heady mix of cigarette smoke, a warm and fruity sort of perfume and strong breath mints. "Well Richard, I see you're still driving around in a time machine.", she said, like she was giving me marks out of ten. However, I was quick with a cheeky reply, "Where are we off to then, Tina, 1977?". That really annoyed her though and she pretended to punch me in the balls. "Sorry Tina, I didn't mean that. You look wicked! I was only messing about. You know what I'm like.", I apologised, as I reversed off the kerb. "Do you wanna pick a tape?", I asked her, nodding my head down to the cassette drawers under the radio. The Nova has black plastic holders for 5 tapes, with white plastic eject buttons.

"What is this then, a lucky dip?", Tina asked me. That's the problem with the cassette drawers, you can't actually see the tapes that are inside them. I answered, "Yes Tina, it's a lucky dip. I live a very exciting life. If you ever need me, you'll find me...". "...at the very edge!", Tina finished my sentence without missing a beat. I couldn't really believe that the old Tina I knew from years ago was back and that other version of Tina, the boring one with a supply teacher vibe, was gone. She pressed the little white plastic button to the right of the middle cassette drawer, lifted out the tape and attempted to scan the label in what little light there was inside the car. "I can't read it, Richard.", she said as she handed me the cassette. I tilted it towards the light coming in from the Indian takeaway and read, "Moby. Everything Is Wrong.". "I know how he feels.", Tina quipped as she swiped the tape from my hand and slipped it into the player. I raised the volume until I could hear the gentle hissing noise before Hymn began to play. "So, where do you want to go to Miss Tina?", I asked. "Let's go up to the reservoir.", she answered, before lighting a cigarette.

"Did you notice that my motor had a new car smell before you lit up?", I enquired. Tina's eyes scanned back and forth across the dashboard before replying, "This car wasn't even new when you bought it, Richard! I can't imagine your clothes were either. Nike Air Max 90, popper tracksuit bottoms and a Spliffy hoodie? It's just as well we're driving up to the reservoir tonight and not going to a restaurant.". I pulled away from the shops and drove slowly towards the ring road while I adjusted my crumpled clothing in an attempt to look slightly more presentable before remarking, "You're starting to sound like my Mum. If you're aiming to pull off that outfit then you'll need to stay in character. We need Punk Tina tonight.". "If I've gone to the effort of sneaking out of my street wearing fishnet stockings then I can assure you that I haven't been thinking of pulling them off myself.", she turned her face towards mine and winked in an over the top and very comical way. "Yes, that's the spirit!", I shouted as I reached my left hand over and squeezed her right thigh. Tina rolled her window down slightly before flicking some cigarette ash into the night.

There's a cinematic sadness to Hymn, the opening track on Moby's 1995 album Everything Is Wrong. The music seemed to drift around the Nova in time with the little swirls of smoke coming from Tina's cigarette. I began to think that I should tone down the playfulness a little, So, I asked her, "How is Mister Short doing these days?". Tina flicked the cigarette butt out of her window, rolled it up, and then started to rummage through the contents of her tiny handbag, "Oh, you know Tony. He's been really busy at work, as usual. Quite stressed. He gets angry sometimes, but mostly he's just really quiet. If I'm honest, I'm glad he'll be away for a few days. I don't know if I'm having a midlife crisis, or whatever, but I met up with our Mandy. You remember our Mandy?", she asked. "How could I forget her?!", I shook my head. Tina laughed, "Well, my rather eccentric older Sister is quite similar to you, Richard, in that she's never really grown up.". "That's a good thing, Tina.", I stated. The contents of her bag was now, mostly, in her hands. A packet of cigarettes, a lighter, a lipstick, a small bottle of perfume and her purse. She opened her purse.

Tina paused briefly and looked at the road ahead. "Mandy, not surprisingly, told me that I needed to do something dangerous, something exciting, or else I'd just become more and more depressed.", she said, before turning her face towards mine. I met her eyes and informed her, "It's a downward spiral.". Tina lifted a small bag of pills out of her purse and began to wave it around between us. "Mandy has been to more festivals this year than I have been to in my entire life. She told me that the playlist on my phone was so embarrassing that if I died before her she would make sure none of it would be played at my funeral as it would bring more shame on the family than the New Year's Day she shat herself on the porch and fell asleep.", Tina laughed. "What on Earth was on your playlist?", I asked. "Normal stuff. I don't know. Adele, Phil Collins, Fleetwood Mac.", she looked towards the tape player. "Fleetwood Mac are good, but it's all about the context. I'm guessing Mandy gave you those pills?", I nodded towards the little bag. Tina put a pill in her mouth and swallowed it. Then she placed one in my left hand and turned up the volume.

The euphoric cacophony of Feeling So Real filled the car as we approached the turn off to the Ring Road. I hadn't gulped a pill in several years, and I'd never taken one while driving. It must have only taken a couple of seconds for me to decide that I was going to eat it, but at the time it felt like I had thought it all over quite well. It takes a while before the effects of ecstasy kick in after necking a pill and I reckoned I'd have plenty of time to get us up to the reservoir while still feeling normal. As long as I drove sensibly I presumed that everything would be fine. I did put my foot down a little bit as we drove onto the Ring Road though. I could feel the huge sub-bass from Moby's track vibrating the motor and for a moment I wondered if Tina could feel it too. As the street lights began to look like they were fluttering past the car like an endless stream of low flying, illuminated, birds, I felt Tina's right hand on my left leg. She wasn't moving it about, rubbing or clawing. Her hand just felt steady. The only time she turned the volume down as we drove towards the reservoir was to ask me if I was wearing Lynx Africa. She smiled when I told her I was.

The reservoir is quite near my place, on a hill that overlooks the city. I've been going up there at night for years as it's so quiet and the view is amazing. By the time I'd parked the car Moby was long gone and we were halfway through Side A of The Prodigy Experience. "Wind It Up was the first single I ever bought. I got it on vinyl. We Are The Ruffest was the B-Side.", I said as I nodded towards the cassette player. "It sounds so fast now. It's good though, I'm buzzing.", Tina replied while tapping her knees and moving her head in time with the beat. "I'm glad I brought some chewing gum with me tonight, I'm rushing here!", I shouted before popping a piece of gum into my mouth and handing the packet over to Tina. "Cool. Cheers. Nice One.", she remarked, squeezing a piece onto her left hand before dropping the remainder of the packet into the little tray in front of the gear stick. My arms felt all tingly and sensitive. I could feel it all over my face too, like I had pins and needles. It reminded me of playing football when I was a kid, drenched in sweat and being blasted by a cold wind. Chewing the gum stopped me from sucking on my lips.

It took a while for my eyes to adjust to the darkness outside the car. I could see a little amber glow dancing on the surface of the reservoir and beyond that the lights that mapped out the city streets seemed to bounce around every time I moved my head. "Tina, I'm flying here! What sort of pills did Mandy give you?", I asked. "Cherries. I've got 9 of them. Well, 7 now.", Tina replied. "I'm not taking 3 of those. No chance. I'm off my tits already! We're walking down to my place from here. There's no way I'm driving.", I gazed at Tina, aware that my eyes were wide open. She smiled and sang, "Too far gone!". I burst out laughing, then I closed my eyes and began to claw at my thighs as Hyperspeed (G-force Part 2) by The Prodigy began to flow out of the speakers and drift into my brain. Tina lowered the volume gently before speaking in her teacherly voice, "We're going to need some water, Richard.". "I've got water!", I enthused, "It's in the boot of the car, in my emergency bag. I'll get it now.". As I stepped out of the Nova I could feel that my entire body was buzzing. I danced my way around to the boot before I gazed up at the stars.

If you drive an old motor then it's a good idea to keep an emergency bag in the boot in case you break down. Every 6 months, or so, I check the contents of mine to make sure that the torch is still working and the food is in date. I was having a bit of difficulty remembering what I was supposed to be looking for and my usual neat and careful ways were set aside as I tipped the contents of the entire bag into the boot. "Jackpot!", I yelled, as a 2 litre bottle of water and a 4 pack of energy drinks landed on top of a bundle of warm clothing. "Nice one, Richard!", Tina shouted from inside the car. I really liked the feeling of lifting the bottle of water as it was covered in condensation. I just about resisted the urge to hug it and rub it all over my face. I picked up the pack of energy drinks, shut the boot, and made my way back to the driver's door. It was then that I noticed that Tina had changed the tape to Behaviour by The Pet Shop Boys, removed her denim jacket and boots, and was now stretched out across both seats. I leaned into the Nova, handed the bottle of water to Tina, who smiled and nodded, and placed the energy drinks in the footwell.

As the track Being Boring lifted towards its first chorus I yelled, "Turn It Up!", and Tina obliged. I started to strip off my hoodie like I was in some sort of failed boy band and I could hear Tina laughing. I twisted my hips and spun around, then I wiggled my ass into the car until it was kicked. I was laughing my head off before my big reveal. "Wait until you see THIS!", I shouted into the air. "Oh no, don't!", Tina screamed, as I pulled my hoodie over my head to display my Global Hypercolor T-shirt. I popped my smiling face into the car and Tina was holding her belly and laughing uncontrollably. I threw my hoodie into the back seat and climbed into the Nova, lifting Tina's feet up temporarily so that I didn't crush them under my ass. "Aye, the old ones are the best.", I said, as I squeezed her left knee. "Where did you get that relic, Richard? I thought you were going to unpop your popper tracksuit bottoms!", Tina grinned. "One step at a time, my dear! You can get everything online these days.", I replied. "Wow! Mister Nineties is online?", Tina remarked. "Yes, Punk Girl, I'm online. The Pet Shop Boys are brilliant. I'm loving this!", I smiled.

Tina popped another pill into my mouth, which I washed down with energy drink, and she gulped one too with the aid of a mouthful of water. "Pills just taste like headache tablets, really. Folk used to go on about them tasting like hairspray, but no one eats hairspray.", Tina informed me. "They are pretty rough if they get caught in your throat. I had such a dry mouth at one of the early Raves that I thought I was going to choke on a pill. Your Mandy handed me a quarter bottle of whisky and I took a huge gulp. I could hardly see anything because my eyes were streaming with tears and then she smooched me and told everyone it was the kiss of life!", I recounted. Tina shook her head, "Brilliant! You know, Mandy and I haven't seen eye to eye over the years, if I'm honest. She thought I was stupid marrying the only man I'd ever slept with, but she's always been there for me. She was really crazy back in the old Rave days. She's calmed down a bit now, but only a little. I mean, she's just handed me a bag of pills!". "I still can't believe they built a supermarket where we used to Rave. The main stage is now a bakery. It's so sad.", I sighed.

This Must Be The Place I Waited Years To Leave began playing and Tina and I paused to gaze out over the lights of the city. I could feel my body becoming overwhelmed and confused with what it needed to do physically. That can happen whenever pills start to tingle inside your belly. Sometimes you're not sure if you need to go to the toilet, kiss someone, dance, have sex or simply run your fingers around your head and close your eyes. I realised that I was doing the last of these things when I felt Tina's lips kissing mine. I kept my eyes closed as we smooched softly and slowly. My right hand found the side of her face and I tucked her hair behind her ear and pulled the back of her neck towards me. Her right hand was slowly massaging my chest and I could feel my mouth tightening into a smile, wondering if all of this activity was changing the colour of my T-shirt. I should have been alarmed that the wife of my old dropping mate was now sucking on my upper lip, but I was so high that all I could really think about was how silly clothing is, and how funny people are, and how sore my erection was under the weight of Tina's hip.

Strange reversing noises and haunted pads tickled my ears as Tina pulled her head away from mine and the song To Face The Truth began. She ran her right index finger down the length of my nose and placed it on my lips whilst tilting her head back and closing her eyes. "Tony is a leg man, which is just as well because I have no tits.", Tina told the sunroof. I softly bit through her T-shirt in the direction of her right nipple then yelled, "Found one!". Tina opened her eyes and smiled at me, "I'm sorry, I know I shouldn't have mentioned Tony. I think that might have ruined the moment, but I did enjoy it.". "You enjoyed me locating a tit?", I asked. Tina's eyes narrowed as she smirked, "The moment, Richard. I enjoyed the moment.". My right hand searched for her left palm before our fingers interlocked, while my other hand located the volume knob and lowered it to silence. Tina lurched forward and found my left earlobe with her mouth. I could feel the heat of her breath, her tongue moving, and the change in temperature as her saliva cooled. "I want you inside me.", she breathed, ahead of reaching over to open up the driver's door.

"Tina, I'm asexual.", I stated. "You're a sexual what?", Tina asked, as she released my right hand before pulling the door handle. I grasped my chest for comfort, lowered my eyes, and spoke, "I'm asexual. I think I always have been, to some extent.". Tina looked puzzled, "Mandy told me you slept with her last week!", she declared. "I haven't slept with anyone in years, Tina. Never mind last week.", I informed her. "You know what I mean Richard! I'm sorry. What I meant was that I met up with our Mandy last week. My head has been a mess recently. Of course, Mandy's idea of sorting my head out involved getting high and having sex with anyone other than Tony. She suggested several men and I began to feel ill. Then I mentioned you, because I've always liked you. Not in a boyfriend way, but in a close way. I guess, like a friend, in that I can trust you.", she told me, lifting my face up so that our eyes met. "Yes, we are good friends Tina and you can totally trust me. I feel really relaxed with you and I'm having a lovely night. That's part of the problem really. I never feel the same with people after sex. It upsets me. It makes me feel sad.", I confessed.

Tina pushed the door open and looked out into the night, "I need some air.", she said. "You'll need to put your boots back on first.", I pointed out as I squeezed her stockinged feet. "I was going to give you a foot job. I'm something of an expert, Richard.", Tina turned her face towards mine to reveal a cheeky smile. "You can't give a foot job to an asexual, Tina. It's against the rules.", I joked. "I can feel your hard on!", Tina stated as she bounced once, rather theatrically. "Hey, that hurt! You got lucky there, actually. Ecstasy can make a lot of things feel better, but it can be something of a penis disabler. So, Mandy's plan certainly wasn't flawless.", I declared. Tina shuffled her way over to the passenger seat and began to put on her boots. "I don't understand why you have an erection if you don't want to have sex.", she said, sounding baffled. I answered, "My body can still be aroused from time to time and sometimes I masturbate to get rid of it, but I never want to actually have sex with another person. Sometimes I can even become sexually repulsed. I feel awkward if other people are talking about it, or if it's on TV, or whatever.".

"Do you think you are gay?, Tina asked while adjusting her stockings. "No, there's nothing there. I mean, when I think of men there's nothing. It's like thinking about paper-clips or a cooking pot. I'm definitely attracted to women.", I informed her. Tina began to tap the gearstick while looking straight ahead. After a few moments she took a deep breath and turned to face me. "OK Richard, I do appreciate what you're saying, and I know that you haven't had the easiest life, relationship wise, and you are a sensitive soul. However, as a good friend, and considering that you currently have an erection, I would like to have sex with you. That's why I'm wearing stockings and no knickers. It's also why these little boobs that I have are drenched with perfume. So, my darling boy. My beautiful, gorgeous, friend. Please, oh pretty please...", Tina fluttered her eyes as her face moved towards mine, "Fuck me!". I giggled, then my giggle became a laugh. Tina also giggled, but as she did her left hand tickled its way along my thigh until her fingers found the outline of my cock. I leaned forward and lifted the bar to let my seat fall gently backwards.

"Smooth operator.", Tina sang playfully, as she began to open the buttons along the side of my tracksuit bottoms. "I think I should just slide them off, Tina. I don't fancy the angle I would need to be at for my dick to make its way out towards you from below my left pocket.", I said, as my right thumb made it's way beneath my waistband and began to lower my tracksuit bottoms and boxer shorts in a single manoeuvre. Unfortunately, the elasticated belt acted like a sort of slingshot and propelled my knob in such a way that it slapped off my stomach. Tina laughed, "At least my source was correct on one count. You are a big boy!". "Tina, that's exactly the kind of talk that puts me off. Anyway, I thought girls didn't talk about that sort of thing.", I muttered. Tina began to stroke my manhood slowly whilst moving her face towards mine. Then she whispered, "Richard. Dick, if I may. You're in safe hands now. Of course girls talk, and crazy sisters even more-so. Although, since you are being so kind and thoughtful, I promise I'll be quiet for at least the next few minutes.". She kissed her way down my body until her warm mouth enveloped my prick.

Having an erection feels a bit like sustaining a throbbing pain that needs to be soothed and, undoubtedly, a blow job, whilst poorly named, works remarkably well to provide good relief. I find it difficult to focus my thoughts during any kind of sexual activity though. Sometimes I can do quite well if I manage to live in the moment, fully focussed on sexy ideas and feelings. I think that's probably how other people must live most of the time. My mind usually drifts away fairly quickly though, to a point at which I feel almost like an observer. As if I have actually left my body and I'm sort of looking down on whatever it is I'm doing. The way that people who have near-death experiences describe hovering above themselves and gazing down at the operating table. Whenever my thoughts drift out there then I begin to think of how weird sex is. If I'm with a long-term partner then I begin to work out how many times I'm going to have to do this sort of nonsense before I die. Then I start thinking about death. That's a big one, thinking about death. In my head, dying as soon as possible seems much better than having sex for years and years.

"Are you OK, Richard?", Tina asked. My cock was now soaking wet and starting to feel cold in places. "Yeah. Yeah, I'm fine. That felt nice.", I replied, rather faintly. "You're really quiet. No moaning or groaning. At least you aren't giving me orders or saying stupid things like we're in a porn film. You are OK though, yeah?", she looked genuinely concerned. I pulled her up along my body and kissed her slowly. I did the best that I could, a passionate performance, and then I informed her that, "I won't come. I never do. Well, I can make myself come, but it takes ages. I'd rather sit a maths exam than put myself through the ordeal of trying to climax. The good news, from your perspective, is that I can maintain an erection for hours, if required. I also know how to stimulate your G-spot and clitoris.". "This is starting to sound a bit medical, Richard. A bit too scientific.", Tina rested her forearms on my chest. "Sorry. Well, tell me what you had hoped would happen tonight when you got dressed earlier, but decided not to wear pants.", I turned my right ear towards her mouth. "That I'd be shagged from behind across your bonnet, Richard.", Tina grinned.

A few minutes later I was engaged in the business of wish fulfilment and, much to my embarrassment, Tina was a lot more vocal than me, and most porn stars I'd imagine. It did feel nice being inside her and I enjoyed caressing her naked bum. I'd always liked the look of Tina's ass. I apologise if my descriptions of sexual activities drift off the boil every now and then, but that's just as it is in my brain. Whenever I felt Tina's right hand reaching between her legs to gently squeeze my balls I was delighted for a couple of reasons. Firstly, I really enjoyed the warmth. Secondly, I knew that she would soon be bringing herself to the point of orgasm. So, all I had to do was thrust my hips back and forth, varying the speed and angle in order to appear suitably engaged in the process. That then freed my mind up to concentrate on a little satellite that was making it's way through the clear night sky. All I could think about was how stupid the pair of us must look from space and how ridiculous life is. I felt a bit sad when I thought that, perhaps, this was as good as it gets. Then Tina pushed herself back into me hard, shuddered, and fell silent.

I forced my hips forward as hard as I could, momentarily, before withdrawing my member from Tina's pussy. I quickly bent forward and softly bit her right buttock as she giggled and wriggled. As my mind began to wonder if I should kneel down and return the friendly favour of oral sex, she lowered her red tartan skirt and turned to face me. "Thank you, Richard. I feel much better after that.", she smiled at me as she grasped my tool with her right hand and began to stroke it. "Now, what can I do for you?", she asked. I thought about it briefly as I turned my face to look out over the lights of the city. "You could give me a cigarette.", I answered, as I stepped backwards. "Am I that unattractive?", Tina asked, before walking towards the passenger door. "You're gorgeous.", I assured her. "Then, what's the deal?", she enquired, opening the car door in search of her cigarettes and lighter. "The deal is that I'm asexual. Well, maybe I'm demisexual, in that I can have sex with someone I have an emotional bond with. Although, I'd much rather not have sex at all. There are asexual people who have kids. It's a complex area.", I replied.

Tina placed a cigarette between her lips, closed her eyes, lit it and inhaled. She then tilted her head back and exhaled towards the stars. "There are too many labels these days.", she said as she handed me the smoke. I closed my eyes while I took a large drag and thought. As the smoke filled my lungs I remembered why I had quit puffing years ago. "I was really happy to discover those particular labels. For most of my adult life I thought that there was something wrong with me, and me alone. I now know that I'm part of a community of people who's thoughts about sex align with my own. We even have a flag.", I informed her. Tina took the cigarette back from me, as it was clearly unwanted, then said, "I guess that's cool. I feel pretty weird now though, like I've been rejected.". I made my way around to the driver's side and lifted another energy drink whilst stating, "That's why I think sex is always a bad idea. The Comedown is forever and the high is brief.". "Can't sex just be a bit of fun?", Tina asked. "Probably, but not here. I'm too invested in everything. From music to relationships, it's all or nothing for me.", I answered.

I knew that there was now more than just the width of the car between the two of us and I think Tina could feel that too. "One more for the road?", she asked. My jaw ached and the inside of my cheeks felt like they were going to take days to heal up, but my vision was back to normal. "Yes.", I nodded. We each swallowed a final pill and Tina handed me the little bag with the 3 remaining Cherries. Tina slipped on her denim jacket, gathered her things, and managed to fit them all into her tiny leather bag. "Do you need anything warmer to wear, Tina? I've got loads of clothes here.", I asked her as I fumbled through the items strewn around the boot. "No, I'll be fine. It's not too far to your place from here. I'm glad I wore boots though, rather than heels.", she looked down at her feet. "Yes, good call. I've got a torch here to help us find our way down to the main road.", I said, "We can use the lights on our phones, Richard.", Tina replied, as she began to play, With A Little Bit Of Luck by DJ Luck and MC Neat on her smartphone. I slipped my hoodie over my head and locked up the Nova before I took Tina's hand and we made our way down the hill.

We both decided that it would be a good idea to pee before we reached the bright lights of the main road. Tina squatted and began to relieve herself immediately, joking that she might leave her house without wearing knickers more often. I stood, for what felt like an eternity, with my cock in my hand and not a drop of piss forthcoming. Although, whenever the urine eventually began to flow it felt heavenly. "This is better than sex!", I shouted into the trees that were swaying gently in the darkness before me. "Thanks Richard. You're doing wonders for my confidence tonight.", Tina quipped. I shook myself dry then turned around. "I suppose you'll not want to take my hand again after that?", I asked. "You'd be correct, Richard. Anyway, now that we're heading back into civilisation, it's best that we go back to being friends.", Tina replied, as we both began to walk towards the first of the street lights that would guide us back to my place. The act of lowering ourselves into the city seemed to signal a change in our mood. As the final Cherries of the night began to tingle in our bellies I could sense us shift towards a feeling of contemplation.

"I'm never over at this side of town now." Tina informed me. "I can't believe how small the gates of our high school look. I remember them being huge, but I guess it's because I was just a kid back then.", she continued. "I drive around here all the time. So, I guess I'm used to how the school looks. It's the old farm that bothers me.", I confessed, as the vast supermarket car park came into view. "I can remember when I was a kid my Mum told me that a field she used to play in when she was a child was now a biscuit factory. She seemed sad about it, but I told her that I liked biscuits and she laughed. I suppose we would just sound like crazy old people if we began talking about how we miss an old farm that was here when we were teenagers, because that's were all the best Raves were held.", Tina giggled. "Yes, I guess we are old people now.", I said. "It honestly doesn't feel like that long ago that Tony and I were dancing through the night up here, with the pupils in our eyes looking like they'd been sketched by a cartoonist.", I considered. "It feels like ages ago to me, unfortunately. Tony has been completely dry, and boring, for years.", Tina grumbled.

"I can remember the first night Tony and I dropped together. I didn't really know what was going to happen. I was pretty scared, actually. Your Mandy was in the field, sharing a joint with her friend, Nicola, and gazing at the lights in the sky and around the fairground rides. She told us to go and dance in the barn, or else we'd just end up spaced out and boring the pair of them by talking nonsense.", I said. "Fair point though. You don't really want to be babysitting a couple of gurning kids when you're stoned.", Tina stated. "We thought it was quite uncharitable of them at the time, actually. Anyway, Tony and I danced off into the barn and it was absolute chaos in there. There were girls sucking on dummies, lads blowing whistles, smoke machines, strobe lights and this huge, green, laser that seemed to be swallowing up the whole dance floor.", I enthused. "Dance floor? I think you mean straw and cow shit, Richard.", Tina laughed. "Then the DJ mixed in What Time Is Love by The KLF, the Pure Trance version. First time I ever heard it. I thought that the aliens had arrived to join the party. Close Encounters Of The Rave Kind!", I smiled.

I pulled out my phone and searched for The KLF with my eyes bouncing all over the place. "I've got pure flickery vision here, Tina. That last pill is going to end me.", I chuckled. "I can feel it tickling my arms and across my forehead.", Tina briefed me. "Well, since you're such a big fan of Mandy's advice, I guess we should go and dance in the barn!", I pressed play on What Time Is Love and we bounded down a little grass embankment and onto the empty car park. "If you move your head around fast the lights look better!", Tina shouted as she danced, her hands raised above her head and her hips squirming. I wiggled my fingers in front of my eyes as I looked up at the white lights above the car park. "Amazing!", I confirmed, before dancing in circles around Tina as she moved in perfect time with the beat. "If you close your eyes you can sort of get there. Try to find the party.", I garbled, my words drifting out of my mouth almost in the wrong order. As the track reached its climax I could feel Tina's hands on my face. "Look, Richard! Look!", she shouted over the music as her hands turned my face towards a distant sunrise.

The sun was up by the time we were sneaking into my street, looking like a pair of kids who had been out all night throwing eggs at windows. As I ushered Tina into my living room she informed me that, "This place never changes.". I pointed out that, "The decks are new and I got rid of the bean bag chair that followed me from house to house since I was 15.". Looking towards my shelving units she said, "I meant that you still buy 2 copies of everything, Richard. It's very odd behaviour.". "It's traditional behaviour, actually. I have a copy that I use and a perfect copy that I keep in mint condition. My Granny would be proud.", I announced as I made my way towards my vinyl collection, in search of 76:14 by Global Communication. "They'll all end up in the same skip whenever you die. Everything is digital now and this is all just clutter.", she announced, as her hands seemed to gesture towards everything in the room. I located the record and placed the final side upright on the nearest turntable as Tina made herself comfortable on my swivel chair. I dropped the needle onto the vinyl, then I closed my eyes as 12:18 began.

Tina apologised, "I'm sorry I was so harsh on you there, I didn't mean to be. You've always been unique, Richard. Weird, but in a good way.". I lifted the little wooden box that I keep my weed in and made my way towards the sofa to use my bong. As I sat down and opened the lid of the box Tina asked, "Richard?". Whenever I looked towards her she uncrossed her legs slowly, like Sharon Stone in the film Basic Instinct, then whispered, "Can you forgive me?". As my eyes widened I spoke, "I suppose I could overlook your...". "Vulva?", Tina laughed, before crossing her legs. "Mandy will be happy that I have now slept with more than 1 person in my sheltered life.", she continued. I shook my head as I inspected the water. I then began to flake some grass into the bud bowl. "Can't we just keep that to ourselves?", I asked. "Girls talk, Richard, and crazy sisters even more-so. Anyway I feel good about it.", Tina leaned back on the chair, her right foot gently rocking it from side to side. I listened to the blissful music as I closed the box and began to search for my lighter. "I don't feel so good about it.", I confessed.

Tina stood up, opened up her tiny handbag and lifted out the lighter before walking across the room to join me on the sofa. I continued, "I know I don't keep in touch with Tony any longer, but he's still a mate. I've been trying to think about how I feel about old friends that I'm no longer in contact with. It's maybe similar to the way I think about past girlfriends. Well, not from relationships that ended badly, but the ones were we just outgrew each other. I know there's no place in my life for them now, but I still think about them sometimes and hope that they're doing well. That's probably the way I think about Tony, but instead of wishing him well I've just shagged his wife.". Tina handed me her lighter as I lifted the bong to my mouth and covered the clutch hole. While I began to burn the weed and inhale Tina massaged the top of my head with the fingers of her right hand. She moved forward and kissed my cheek as I uncovered the hole and smoke filled my lungs. As I closed my eyes to absorb the moment I felt completely at peace. Right then I felt content, like I was home. Not sitting in my living room home, but spiritually home.

The Comedown began the moment I exhaled. It felt like I had breathed my soul out of my body and I was suddenly empty inside. I looked around my living room and I knew that Tina was right. All of my precious belongings would soon be landfill and I would be dead. There were losses to be endured before that though. Tina would soon be leaving. Returning to her marital home after a little holiday in my misery. I started to think about seeing Grandad in his coffin in the middle of the good room. Then I began to imagine lying in my own coffin, in my living room, surrounded by clutter with no air in my lungs. My face felt cold and numb. My body was shaking. "Richard, you're having a white-out. I'll get you some water.", Tina declared as she took the bong and lighter from my hands. She seemed to be gone for a long time. I could hear the needle on the turntable drifting endlessly around the run-out groove of the record. I tried to focus my eyes on the shelves across the room, but they kept floating past each other, from left to right, on a loop. I gazed at the floor and focussed all of my attention on not vomiting. It worked.

"Sorry Tina, I'm wiped here.", I mumbled as she handed me a pint of cold water. "It's fine Richard, The Comedown has arrived. What goes up must come down. I'm going to tell Tony I have the flu whenever he gets back.", she said whilst lifting the needle off the record. Little sips of water were all I could manage and, as my talk dried up, Tina began playing with her phone. "Time for me to hit the road, Richard. I'm ordering a cab. Hopefully I'll be home before my neighbours are awake. I'm a little too old for the walk of shame.", she smiled. The room was slowly spinning, so I closed my eyes. Little Lies by Fleetwood Mac began to drift out from Tina's phone and it made me feel so low that I wanted to cry. Reality was on the way and I was born to dream of better places than The Real World. I guess that most people must think that Rave is something to dance to at the weekend. For me, Rave is a way of life. As the song ended Tina rose to her feet and announced, "That's my taxi, Richard. Thanks for last night. If you ever need me you'll find me...". "...at the very edge!", I shouted, raising my glass in honour of the madness.

Soon after Tina had closed my front door I crawled onto the rug in the middle of my living room and listened to an hour long version of Rhubarb by Aphex Twin. My thoughts were unfocussed, but depressing. I felt embarrassed about identifying as asexual. I wasn't sure if my life had any purpose or meaning. I missed Tina, but I also missed Tony. Well, I missed who Tony used to be. My forehead felt cold and my body trembled. Whenever the music reached a quiet section I could hear my heart beating. I focussed on my breathing in an attempt to calm down. The white-out passed, eventually, and I made my way to the bathroom and splashed cold water on my face. Then I made the mistake of looking at myself in the mirror. A strange part of getting old is that I feel the same on the inside as I always have done. So, I presume that the World is looking at the same version of me that it saw whenever I was 19, or 27. Instead, I find a caricature of my face looking out at me from inside mirrors that looks more like my Grandad than any teenager or twenty-something. It's a reminder that my body grew up despite my youthful mindset.

I still go to clubs and Raves, but I can only handle a big night out a few times a year now. I've also got no choice but to take my elderly face with me for the ride. I'm still the first on the dance floor though. I arrive thinking that the young people must think I look like an undercover cop, a taxi driver, or someone's angry Father, but all of that speculation dissolves as soon as I get lost in the music. The beats are still as good as ever and the crowds remain beautiful. Anyone informing you that things were better during some golden era is more likely to be mourning their youth than the loss of some obscure drum pattern or venue. Modern lights and visuals combined with a kick drum assault that will physically move you is capable of taking you anywhere you want to go. The limitations on our lives are often self-imposed. The kid's are alright. There is a new generation who know that Techno is still the future. Unlike the youth movements that came before it, House music has never been surpassed. Rave isn't something with a funny haircut in a faded magazine. You can find it at a festival, or in a club, near you tonight.

The weeks between studying my ageing reflection in that bathroom and gazing into the mirror of this mustard Nova this morning have been difficult ones. The Comedown to end all comedowns. Decades ago I would have washed away the Blues after my wild night with Tina by drinking my way towards another crazy weekend. Along with crippling backache, age brings wisdom. My body simply couldn't take that sort of relentless hammering now. The KLF once claimed that Kylie Said To Jason, "It's all in the mind.". I think Kylie might have been onto something. Not long after Tina had sent me a message to tell me she got home safely, I found myself thinking that I could no longer deal with other people. I lay down on my bed for a while, but I couldn't sleep. My head was in a really bad place. I turned off my phone and slipped it under the pillow, then I started to bundle clothes into black plastic bags. That's what I filled this Nova up with at first, clothes and bedding. It was only last week that I came up with the idea of filling the black plastic bags with balloons. They're lighter, so it made more sense at the time.

The bags filled with balloons form a physical barrier between me and the rest of the World. No one would see a car filled up with bags and ask for a lift. That has been my reasoning up until now. This morning is different though. After weeks of ignoring phone calls and gazing through old friends in traffic, I feel like I'm ready to rejoin the party. It's time to replace the thousand-yard stare with an engaging smile. What I've learned about drugs and alcohol is that they create a constant cycle of celebration and hiding. After decades of existing like that I'm ready to try something new. Clean living. Coffee and doughnuts. That's why I'm parked up outside the supermarket at five in the morning, I read online that the doughnuts are freshly baked before the store opens. They have a coffee machine here too. I'm going to get a large vanilla latte and a box of doughnuts and then I'm heading home to have a shower and a shave. After that, I'm going to get dressed in my Levi 501's, Reebok Pump and No Fear hoodie and I'm taking my good Nova out for a spin. Glacier white with 3 spoke alloys. That car turns heads, and I'm in the right mood to go out in it.

I've worked out what I need to do to fix myself. This morning I'm sitting in my mustard yellow Nova with grey wheel trims, in the dark, with my earplugs in, the windows rolled up, the sunroof wound down and all the other seats loaded up with black plastic bags filled with balloons, and I'm holding a knitting pin. The supermarket car park is almost empty. I guess the few motors that are here belong to the night shift staff. I wonder if any of the older ones used to Rave here, and I hope that the younger ones know the way to the after-party. Today I will become The Lone Raver. I will say things without talking and I will represent my tribe, just like that Teddy Boy who used to stand around street corners up the town did. That guy made an impression on me. There's always a reason why you feel drawn to things. It's usually because whatever it is that has caught your eye is mirroring something inside you. Soon I will be playing the Hi-Lo Remix of Skyscrapers by Nina Kraviz and bursting balloons. Shortly after that I will be eating doughnuts. Then I will drive up to the reservoir and spin doughnuts with my good Nova. That car turns heads.

02. DEATH NOTES

Helen Sutherland sat down at the foot of her double bed and gazed at her reflection in one of her two mirrored wardrobes. The young man at the bedroom furniture store had told Helen that mirrored wardrobes would make her bedroom look bigger. After living with these wardrobes for over a year Helen had come to the conclusion that they made her face, bum and tummy look bigger too. Most days Helen wanted to smash her mirrored wardrobes into tiny pieces. She thought that she could maybe use one of her dining room chairs to do the smashing with, as she hated those too. The chairs made ripping sounds whenever people moved around on them. Her husband, John, had once said that, "Ruth next door will think all we ever do is fart in this room.". It was the thought of Ruth next door hearing mirrored wardrobes being smashed into tiny pieces with a dining room chair that had held Helen back from doing it. Helen hated feeling restrained, watched, judged and controlled all of the time. That's why she lied.

Helen only ever told little lies. She felt that they protected her from the truth and made her feel better. They weren't the sort of lies that could hurt people. Helen thought that Ruth next door probably told those sort of lies to her husband, Tom. Perhaps last Tuesday night when he arrived home from football training half an hour after a skinny man with a moustache left his house by the kitchen door. Yes, Helen was fairly certain that Ruth would have told a big lie then. Compared to that type of lie Helen felt that her little fibs were hardly lies at all. Like telling people that she was 47 rather than 59. As far as she was concerned people were only as old as they felt. Helen might inform someone that she lived in Morningside, rather than Marchmont. Comforting herself with the idea that it might depend upon which way they would drive into her area, if they ever visited. Helen wished her mirrored wardrobe could start telling little lies too. She looked at her reflection and began to think that she should have bought a single full length mirror instead. A skinny one, from a funfair. Helen sighed, then reached out to slide open the wardrobe door.

As the fingertips of her right hand touched the cold surface of the mirror Helen's mood shifted from one of irritation to a sense of sadness. She could colour her hair, powder her face and hide her ageing neck with a scarf, but she knew that her hands looked old. Perhaps not very old, but certainly a lot older than she would like them to look. Helen briefly thought about wearing gloves more often. She wondered if wearing bigger, or smaller, jewellery would help. If her wardrobe wasn't so full she may have toyed with the idea of stepping into it and sliding the door closed behind her forever. She knelt on the bedroom carpet and slid open the wardrobe door as far as it would go. Above her head clothes hung in a highly organised, colour coordinated, fashion. It had taken her all of the previous afternoon to do that, inspired by a segment on morning television. Today Helen was set to tackle the avalanche of shoes at the bottom of the wardrobe. After staring at them for what felt like ten minutes she decided that the best way to do this would be to take them all out of the wardrobe and rearrange them. That's when she noticed an old diary.

It was a small, brown, leatherette bound book with 1974 printed on the front cover in silver ink. Helen guessed that it had fallen out of the dusty shoe box full of memories she had thrown out the day before, after the smell of her late Mother's perfume had made her cry. 1974, she would have been 13 then. Helen smiled as she lifted the diary. She ran her fingers across its cover and blew the dust from the edge of its pages. When she opened the book she giggled at the sight of her handwriting. Helen read her name and her childhood address before mouthing her old telephone number. She could remember her parents answering the phone by reciting it instead of saying "Hello.".

Deciding that the avalanche of shoes could be tackled at a later date, Helen made her way onto the bed and began to read her old diary. January's entries mainly concerned Harvey the dog, the walks she had taken him on, the furniture he had chewed and how it wasn't her fault that she hadn't noticed him chewing those things. Several entries made note of a friend called Tracey, but Helen couldn't remember who she was at all.

February began with her birthday. The notes mentioned new roller skates, a large chocolate cake and a tally of 17 birthday cards. Helen's eyes glazed over as she tried to recall how many cards she had received in recent years. She thought of all the deaths in her family and of the friendships that had faded from her life in the years since she had written the diary. The entry for Valentine's Day only mentioned one card, from a boy named Peter. Helen remembered that he was tall and that he rode a red bicycle, but she couldn't picture his face. The final diary entry had been penned on the evening of the first Saturday in March. Helen had written that whenever she grew up her children would not be given a bedtime or silly rules to follow. After making this note she had abandoned the book and left it to gather dust.

The noise of the garden gate alerted Helen and she made her way to the bedroom window just in time to see Ruth and the skinny man with the moustache walking towards the house. Helen tapped on the glass and smiled and waved at Ruth when she looked up at the window, enjoying the panicked look on her face.

Helen glanced back towards the open wardrobe and was pleased not to be confronted with her reflection. She felt there was a smug sort of smile on her face. The type of smile that she wouldn't want to have confirmed in a mirror. Whilst gazing at her highly organised, colour coordinated, rail of clothing Helen decided that she would simply keep one of her wardrobe doors open at all times. This would half the number of full length mirrors in her bedroom instantly. She fetched a pen from the top drawer of her bedside cabinet and flicked through the last pages of her old diary. Above a section called Notes she wrote the word Death. Helen then scrawled; I have grown up. I have given children bedtimes and silly rules to follow. Harvey the dog died. Daddy died. Mum died too. I can't remember Tracey or Peter. I can remember my old phone number. I married a good man called John. Our daughter, Wendy, has a son named Kyle. I let him stay up past his bedtime and break silly rules. Helen put her old diary and the pen into the top drawer of her bedside cabinet. She then lifted her phone and sent John a text; We deserve better dining room chairs x

03. LIGHTS OUT IN THE BOOTH

We welcome you to Hell Scarlett Young. Your body has travelled through the night to reach us. Due to the success of the Coronavirus pandemic our colleagues at The Morgue have been extremely busy. They have asked us to convey their sincere apologies for any delay in processing your corpse. We are Shadow Sean and Crimson Kate, better known as The Mosquitoes. At night we are a formidable DJ duo, travelling the World to play Techno at the hottest underground clubs. Before dawn breaks we work for an hour here in Hell ahead of retiring to our coffin beds. We are, of course, vampires. You are probably wondering if that pain in your neck is an indication that you are now a vampire too, not yet. As it happens, you were kidnapped, raped, tortured and strangled to death by a serial killer called Bernard Berkley. We will be dealing with Bernard here in Hell as soon as he dies. Until then, The Man Upstairs has asked us to show you the facilities. These are earplugs for DJ's and musicians, wear them and follow us.

As you can see, the walls here in Hell are painted beige, with the exception of our blacked-out sleeping quarters. We have been vampires since we were buried alive by a wild mob at a roadside in rural Sligo during the cholera outbreak of 1832. Like all great epidemics and pandemics it moved from east to west in order to stay ahead of the Sun. Not all vampires are suckers of blood, some dispatch their victims by inflicting upon them infectious diseases. It is those sort of vampires who are currently thriving in the World. You will see many of these MIND YOUR HEAD signs dotted about the place, as decapitation remains the only way to kill any kind of vampire. Whenever we refer to The Man Upstairs it can relate to both God and the Devil. To us, they are interchangeable. They are both about blood lust. All of that, "Eat my flesh, drink my blood.", stuff is very relatable for vampires. Many religious scholars see the vampire as a mirror of Christianity. Those same scholars cannot see us in their mirrors. Those who pray are easy prey. Here, take this gun, it is loaded with silver bullets. We will soon be entering our place of work.

Travis Reid is the man we will be dealing with today. In life, he was an only child. Raised by his Grandmother in her suburban bungalow, he spent much of his time playing with animals in her basement. Travis liked ice cream, comic books and removing the eyes and claws from kittens and puppies. Shortly after the death of his Grandmother, Travis began to murder prostitutes. He killed a dozen women before he was shot and killed by law enforcement. Ever since then he has been in this room. Mind the step. As you can see, Travis is bound and gagged. His hands are cuffed behind his back, securing him to an upright beam. This is the same position each of his victims found themselves in shortly before they were killed. Travis is currently asleep. The closest experience to death that a living human can feel is when they are anaesthetised before an operation. In that state they are no longer a person and their body is merely an object. There is no feeling before birth and there is no feeling after death, unless you become a vampire. We will now ask you to wake Travis up by firing your gun in the direction of his right kneecap.

Well done Scarlett, that was an accurate shot. Travis is now wide awake and in incredible pain. His means of communication are very limited and our earplugs do a sensational job of filtering out unwanted frequencies, like his moans and grunts. We will now dance towards Travis in a happy and jolly manner to the sound of this boy band music. As you can see, he is very confused. Watch his face whilst one of us forces his head back against the upright beam with a foot and the other sucks his right eyeball out of his head and chews it off at the stalk. Travis has fainted in shock. We will now ask you to wake him up by firing your gun in the direction of his left kneecap. Wonderful teamwork everyone, Travis is now awake again and looking around the room with his left eye. It is time for us all to dance our way towards the door. This song never reaches a chorus, by the way. Verses rarely bring any joy to the listener. Travis is terrified of snakes. So, releasing a thirty foot long anaconda above his head by simply pressing this button upon exit is a fantastic way to wrap up our task for the day. We'll give you the honour of pressing it Scarlett.

Working in Hell is very easy, and it can also be fun. Although, we must warn you that we have decades of experience. As vampires, we need to be careful not to ingest dead blood. So, things like sucking out eyeballs can be risky. Torturing murderers like Travis is something we do every day. We like to keep evolving the sequence of events in order to maximise the torment for our subject and keep things fresh for ourselves. As soon as the anaconda has killed Travis that room will return to exactly how it was before we entered it today. People in Hell spend the majority of their time asleep, but they aren't aware of that time passing. Someone like Travis could be asleep for years before we wake them up to kill them again, but they will feel like no time has passed at all since they were last tortured. It's a very clever system. As a vampire, sleeping feels like it takes no time at all. As soon as our coffin lids close they open again. Sometimes we wonder if Heaven exists, or if it operates in a similar way. We don't fear death at all, as we know it will feel like nothing. Just as it did before we were born. We can all now remove our earplugs.

There is a small keypad to the right of the door behind you Scarlett. Beyond this portal are our blacked-out sleeping quarters. Our home, if you will. Please type the number 616 then ENTER, freely and of your own will. Welcome to our humble haven, dear Scarlett. Allow us to light a few candles and let the door close behind you. There are three wonderful coffin beds awaiting our weary bodies. The ground beneath our feet is dusted with Irish earth. It is the soil of our homeland, of your place of birth too Scarlett. We think that now would probably be a good time to tell you more about that pain in your neck. We told you that we are vampires, and that is true. However, after 190 years of shape shifting and blood sucking we are, quite frankly, bored to death of it all. Last week we approached The Man Upstairs to tell him this and he has kindly agreed to let us die a decade from now during a beach party at dawn in Vama Veche, southern Romania. That is where vampires go to perish. We will be beheaded together at 6am while we listen to the music of Maurice Ravel. That leaves us with 10 years to train you as our replacement, dear Scarlett.

Please lower your revolver. We are sure those would have been perfect shots to our heads, Scarlett Young. Alas, your gun was loaded with just two silver bullets, which are now embedded in Travis' knees. We must also inform you that Bernard Berkley does not exist and that, in fact, you were killed by us. We were, however, truthful in telling you that you are not yet a vampire. You are a newborn, and will be for one year. Some vampires would refer to you as a fledgeling, as you have not yet drunk any human blood. We will teach you all we know in the time we have with you and, best of all, you will be able to find a partner to share this home with once we are no more. We advise you to choose wisely, as 200 years is a very, very, long time to spend with anyone. If it makes you feel any better, you rushed towards us because you wanted to die. Sometimes there is a desire for death when one is confronted with it. Police have noted that occasionally cars have accelerated before hitting trees. No one wants to end up on the scrapheap, Scarlett. We promise you that you had a look in your eyes that you will soon see in the eyes of many people.

It is time for us to sleep. We, as The Mosquitoes, have a gig at midnight in Moscow. You, dear Scarlett, are our new tour manager. It is your job to ensure that no House music is played as we enter the club, that there are no mirrors in our dressing room and that the lights are out in the DJ booth as we perform. In time we will teach you to become one with Techno, to feed off the energy in the room, to be repelled by every Raver with drugs in their blood. As the repetitive beats pulse through our bodies you will sense someone being drawn towards you in a state of complete surrender. It will be time for you to make your first kill. This will feel natural, like you have been handed a cold bottle of water after running through the flames of Hell. Follow that feeling. Offer your victim a VIP wristband before you lead them to our dressing room. Although, do remember that they too shall be one of us once your deed is done. So, choose wisely Scarlett. We don't wish to spend a decade training an idiot alongside you. Go for someone who is alluring, charming and seductive. Now though, this coffin bed is yours. Sleep well, dear Scarlett.

04. BEN SMYTH

My name is Ben Smyth. I am 6 years old. I live in Gatehouse. The full name of Gatehouse is Gatehouse Of Fleet. My full name is Ben Stuart Smyth. My dead Grandad was called Stuart and now I have his name in the middle of my name. Mister Brown lives next door. Mister Brown calls me Benjamin but that is not my name. Mister Brown is old and he smells like old people and bad smoke. His house is number 8 and our house is number 6. He gave me a selection box at Christmas but forgot my birthday even when my Mammy put balloons in the window. He is so old.

It is the Summer now and today is a Tuesday. My Mammy makes me sausages and chips with ketchup on Tuesdays but she just eats chips with no ketchup and something else that I would not like. I am sitting on the front steps that Alex is painting the sides of. Alex is a painter sometimes and he can fix cars and one motorbike. Alex is sweating a lot and he is smelly. The new paint smells better than Alex.

Alex said I am Smyth with a Y because I keep asking questions. He is not allowed to read my book. Alex told me not to sit on the steps but I am sitting on the steps. On Sunday Alex said my Mammy asked him to paint the steps so that she can keep up with the Joneses. There are no Joneses living in our street. I asked Mister Brown yesterday and he has lived here for a very long time. Alex does not even live here. He just stayed over on Saturday night. Mister Brown is smarter than Alex and he does not even have a computer. My Mammy bought an old book for Mister Brown from the internet at Christmas and he cried. I am a brave soldier. That is what my Mammy calls me because I did not cry when my Daddy died. I kill all of the big spiders for my Mammy. I told her not to let Alex drink tea from my Easter egg mug again. She said she will not let him. I am going to stand up now and knock on the living room window to make sure that my Mammy can see me. I do that because Mister Brown told me that my Mammy once lost a child. My Mammy is always losing people.

05. FEAR OF FALLING

Ethel Hawkins woke to the sound of white noise blaring out of the radio alarm clock on her bedside table. Until recently the device had been tuned to a Classical station, but Ethel had altered the frequency of the set whilst attempting to increase the volume of The Blue Danube one morning and, ever since, had woken up to blasts of static, white noise or, occasionally, heavily distorted Pop music. Fixing radios was the sort of thing that her late husband, Frank, would have helped her with. He had died of a heart attack two years previously and since then their bungalow had fallen into a state of disrepair. From her bed Ethel could see that the woodchip wallpaper was beginning to peel away from the wall above the window and her navy coloured curtains were cradling a layer of dust in each fold. She switched off her alarm, sat up at the side of her bed, and moved her right foot around slowly in search of her slippers. Ethel thought that her footwear moved about in the night as it never felt easy to locate in the morning.

After rising to her feet Ethel waited a moment for the light-headedness to pass before the pain in her right knee acted as a reminder to take her morning pills. She washed them down with a gulp of water from the glass that rested on her bedside table before making her way to the lavatory. An old box of matches up on the windowsill made her smile. Frank had never smoked, but he would always have burned a match after he had been to the toilet. Ethel kept lots of things around the house that reminded her of Frank. Her favourite was a bottle of Bay Rum that he used to use after his morning shave. Every few weeks, when she remembered it was there, Ethel would unscrew the cap and lift the open bottle up to her nose. The warm smell seemed, almost, to have a hint of menthol at the end of it. That would make her close her eyes and then she could nearly feel Frank giving her a big hug before kissing her forehead. Once she had gone to the loo and brushed her teeth Ethel removed her night shirt and washed her face and armpits with a soapy facecloth. She then dried herself before padding her way back to the bedroom to dress.

Ethel emerged from her bedroom a quarter of an hour later wearing a purple beret, an orange sweater, black trousers and a pair of grey flat shoes. She made her way to the kitchen, switched the kettle on and looked out at the garden. The grass was overgrown and the old coal shed was now completely hidden behind an enormous Butterfly Bush. It was a bright morning in late May and the birds and insects seemed to be enjoying the wild oasis much more than Ethel. While she made herself a cup of tea and popped a couple of slices of bread into the toaster she thought about her finances and wondered if she would be able to afford the services of a gardener any time soon. Money had been very tight ever since Frank had died and Ethel found herself cutting back on a lot of the little things that she enjoyed in life, like bars of chocolate, marmalade for the toast and even sugar for her tea. She couldn't go without milk though, as she felt that black tea left her mouth feeling dry. Ethel knew that the garden was beginning to get out of hand and that it would need to be tackled before anything inside the house was to be freshened up.

The living room looked rather gloomy as Ethel carried her breakfast through to the table by the window. She noticed that her little front garden was in the shade as the sun was up behind the bungalow. Once seated, Ethel watched the local teenagers make their way towards the high school in the next street. If she timed it right, Ethel would be able to make her way to the supermarket and back before the worst of those kids were on their morning break, smoking and spitting to pass the time in the alleyway at the bottom of the lane. The junk mail from the previous day was stacked up on the table and Ethel looked through it as she ate the last of her toast. One brightly coloured leaflet was advertising a lunchtime pizza delivery deal. The price of each pizza listed was almost as much as Ethel would spend on her weekly groceries. There was a flyer announcing a Summer sale on fitted kitchens and a letter, addressed to Frank, from a cancer charity. Ethel decided to use the back of the envelope to write her shopping list on. It took several moments to get the ink in the pen running. Twelve items were listed. She would need her shopper.

Ethel kept her shopping trolley next to Frank's old golf bag in the hallway. She lifted her grey overcoat off the coat rack and slipped it on before feeling the pockets for her purse and house keys. Ethel removed the keys from her pocket and unlocked the dead bolt before twisting the Yale lock and opening the front door. The day felt colder than it looked. So, Ethel fastened the middle few buttons on her overcoat ahead of stepping outside, bumping her shopping trolley down the step behind her. After closing the door Ethel had a look across the street towards number 12. The Connolly's were one of the few families still living in the area from the time that Ethel and Frank had moved in. Jane Connolly had died just before Christmas without giving Ethel her big soup pot back. Ethel felt unable to bring up the subject with Jack Connolly at Jane's funeral, but remained hopeful that he would see her leaving the house one day and wave her over to return the pot. Unfortunately, the living room curtains were still drawn at number 12. So, Ethel made her way down the lane towards the alleyway that led to the school, and the supermarket, in the next street.

Ethel felt that the pain in her knee had been slowing her down recently, and she had never been all that quick on her feet to begin with. This slow pace gave her time to take everything in. Although, it seemed to be mainly broken glass and litter on the pavement that attracted her attention as she shuffled her way along it. She paused for a moment outside the Burke's house at number 3. Ethel knew them well enough to wave if she saw them at the window, and their wooden fence was just the right height for her to lean on for a while. The garden at number 1 was in great shape. A perfect lawn, well kept borders, and yellow roses starting to bloom. Ethel was pleased that one of the newer residents was taking pride in their home. However, it did make her wonder what the neighbours thought about the state of her own garden at present. The sound of a dog barking behind a fence got Ethel moving again and before long she was making her way through the alley. For once her eyes were not drawn towards the illegible graffiti that was sprayed on the walls. Instead, she looked straight ahead at two large cars with blacked-out windows.

There was a racket coming from the direction of the vehicles. It was a mixture of loud music, engine noise, and raised voices. Although, by the time Ethel had reached the end of the alleyway the street was in complete silence. The cars had sped off in opposite directions and there was a full plastic grocery bag in the middle of the road where they had been. As Ethel began to make her way towards the bag a gust of wind caught it and blew some of the contents onto the road, under a parked car, and through the school railings across the street. Ethel couldn't quite believe her eyes when she realised that the bag was filled with cash. The wind blew again, taking more money with it and prompting Ethel to grab the sack of banknotes, unzip her shopping trolley and drop the bulging plastic bag into it. She then began to lift whatever cash she could get to and throw it into her shopper. The money that had blown into the school was now unreachable, as were whatever notes that remained under the parked car after Ethel had gotten down on her knees next to it and swept her right hand around below it, cupping up whatever she could feel.

After standing up again and bundling the loose banknotes into her shopper, Ethel zipped the bag closed and looked up and down the road. There was no one around. Ethel decided that the best thing to do was go home. She wouldn't feel safe going to the supermarket with all of that money in her bag. So, she walked back towards the alleyway with her shopping trolley rattling along the ground behind her. This time she inspected the graffiti to her left. It was bright yellow and Ethel thought that, perhaps, it was supposed to be a shark. "Missus Hawkins?". Ethel looked up towards to top of the alleyway, where the question had came from. A short, bald, muscular man was walking towards her. Ethel thought that he looked quite menacing, like a hard man. Although, he was walking a rather proud looking poodle on a bright pink lead. "Missus Hawkins? I'm Barry The Tank, but that's not what the kids call me around here. I knew Frank, from the club.". "Oh, you're a golfer?", Ethel looked down at the dog, "What's her name?". "Sonia. She's 3.", Barry said, as he pulled on the lead to stop the dog from jumping forwards.

"We saw you out the window there, me and Cheryl. That's my wife, Cheryl. I started whistling Raspberry Beret. You know, the Prince song? Because of your hat like, and Cheryl, the wife, hit me a slap and said you were struggling.", Barry continued while holding Sonia back. Ethel tightened her grip on the shopper, "You saw me out of what window?". "Up there, Missus Hawkins. We're in number 1.", Barry sounded like a child who had lost a football. "Oh, yes. I see. I was stopping to admire your garden. Your roses are beautiful.", Ethel began to relax. "Thanks very much. That's my trade, gardening and landscaping. Keeps me out of trouble. I used to box like, years ago. Barry The Tank Taylor. I was very famous, but not around here.", Barry leaned forward and rubbed Sonia's head, "That's it. Good girl.". The dog moved back and began to sniff around the legs of Barry's blue jeans. "Well, your wife, Cheryl, is right. I am struggling. As you know, I'm a widow now.", Ethel stated. Barry nodded his head sympathetically. "Frank used to look after the garden and it's like a jungle now.", Ethel continued. Barry nodded his head, hopefully.

"Well, since you're out with the dog, you can walk me home and take a look at my overgrown Butterfly Bush.", Ethel declared as she began to trundle forward with her shopping trolley. Barry smiled as he turned around to let Ethel lead the way as Sonia yelped in confusion. "She's thinking we're going home already.", Barry said as he nodded towards Sonia. "You'll have to excuse me, I'm a slow walker these days. My right knee is playing up today. I couldn't even make it to the shop.", Ethel said as she scanned the ground for broken glass. "No worries at all Missus Hawkins, you take your time. I'll tell you what, I'll go to the shop for you once I've had a look at what needs doing with your garden.", Barry suggested. Ethel was pleasantly surprised and asked, "Are you sure? I don't want to put you out.". "I do a lap of the block with the dog anyway. So, I'll be passing the shop. It's no bother. It'll put me in Cheryl's good book too.", replied Barry. Ethel looked towards the living room window as they passed Barry's house and said, "She sounds like a kind-hearted girl.". "Cheryl's a star, and good-looking too!", Barry shouted towards his house.

Ethel paused for a rest outside number 3 again. As she held onto the Burke's wooden fence with her left hand Barry shouted up the street, "We're onto you Sunshine!". Ethel looked up to see one of the cars with blacked-out windows driving slowly past the entrance to the lane. "They're dealing drugs Missus Hawkins.", announced Barry. "Drugs?", replied Ethel. "Our Kyle has started at the high school around the corner there. He's a good lad. I've been trying to get him into the boxing, but he's not interested. He's big into computers.", explained Barry. "Could he take a look at my radio? It's stopped playing music in the mornings.", asked Ethel. "Only in the mornings?", Barry enquired. "Well, I'm not around to hear it during the day.", said Ethel as she let go of the fence and began the final push to get home. "I'll get Kyle to take a look at your radio when we sort out your garden. He helps me out for a few quid at the weekends.", Barry said as he kicked a large stone out of the way of the shopping trolley. "Thanks for that. You can call me Ethel, by the way.", said Ethel. "Alright, Missus Hawkins. I'll call you Ethel.", Barry grinned.

"Anyway, Ethel, Kyle has started at the high school and, like I said, he's a good lad. He must take after Cheryl, because I was up to all sorts of mischief at his age. There's a few troublemakers around here.", Barry stated. "I've seen the broken bottles and the shark.", said Ethel. Barry looked slightly puzzled, but continued, "Kyle told us about that car being parked up outside the school. They're selling drugs to the kids. Hard stuff too, cocaine. So, we're onto them now, me and Cheryl.", said Barry. "What are you going to do?", asked Ethel. "Cheryl wanted to phone the police and describe the car to them, but I told her I'd speak to the school first. The truth is though, I'm going to box the head off the driver one of these mornings.", Barry confessed. Ethel looked over the street. There was still no sign of life at the Connolly house. Ethel briefly considered knocking the door at number 12 to wake up Jack and demand the return of her big soup pot before stating, "Your anger is understandable, Barry. Although, I feel that Cheryl is right. I think you should visit the school on your walk and let them know about the car and the drugs.".

Ethel made her way towards her front door. As she searched for her keys Barry surveyed the front garden. "That's an easy job.", he said. "Wait until you see out the back!", Ethel exclaimed. "Don't you worry yourself. Kyle and I will get it all cleaned up in no time, whatever state it's in. I'm going to need to keep Sonia moving here, we've been a bit slow for her this morning. What is it you need at the shop?", asked Barry. "Oh, I forgot about that. It's very kind of you. Just pick me up some bread and milk. That will keep me going.", replied Ethel as she removed the keys from her pocket and unlocked the dead bolt before twisting the Yale lock and opening the front door. "Bread and milk. Anything else?", enquired Barry. Ethel bumped her shopper up the step, "Oh, go on then. Get me some chocolate, and sugar for my tea.", she said. "I thought you were already sweet enough, Ethel!", joked Barry. Ethel giggled and began to unbutton her grey overcoat. "It might be an hour, or so, before I'm back. I'm going to take your advice and visit the school. Does Saturday morning suit you for the garden?", asked Barry. "Yes, it does.", answered Ethel.

"Come on then!", Barry encouraged Sonia, as they moved off quickly towards the top of the street. Ethel closed the front door and locked the dead bolt before returning the keys to the pocket of her overcoat that they had came from. She then slipped off the coat and hung it up on the rack ahead of wheeling her shopping trolley into the kitchen. After unzipping her shopper, Ethel lifted the bulging plastic bag of cash out and placed it on the table. As she did so several loose notes spun around in the air before landing on the floor. A few minutes of hunting and gathering money later, Ethel was satisfied that it was all on her kitchen table. The overgrown garden provided good cover as she counted the cash, twice. A grand total of £5,270 lay before her in neat bundles. Ethel sized it up before making her way to the big kitchen cupboard and opening it. The bottom shelf was holding up a small sack of potatoes and a plastic bag filled with plastic bags. Ethel scanned the top shelf and lifted out a large box of Corn Flakes and a tin of biscuits. There wasn't much weight in either item and they were easy for Ethel to carry to the table.

Once the bag containing what was left of the Corn Flakes had been lifted out of the box, Ethel realised that all of the cash could be stacked up neatly inside it. There was even enough room left at the top of the box for her to put the bag of Corn Flakes back into. Ethel returned the cereal box to the top shelf of her big cupboard before inspecting the plastic bag that the cash had been in, with a view to putting it into her plastic bag filled with plastic bags. However, she decided that it was too dirty looking to be reused, so she scrunched it up and threw it into her bin. Ethel opened the tin of biscuits, but she wasn't impressed with what remained inside. There were no chocolate ones left. After lifting out a couple of fingers of shortbread, Ethel returned the biscuit tin to the top shelf of her big kitchen cupboard and closed the door. She then placed the shortbread onto a small plate and made her way into the living room. As Ethel walked towards the table by the window she noticed that the shopping list she had made earlier was still there, alongside the brightly coloured leaflet advertising the lunchtime pizza delivery deal.

The living room seemed a little less gloomy now that the sun was beginning to reach the little garden at the front of the bungalow. Once seated, Ethel turned over her shopping list and gazed at Frank's name on the envelope from the cancer charity. Upon opening the pouch, Ethel noticed that it contained a free pen and a letter appealing for a donation to help fund new research. After trying out the pen on the front of the envelope, Ethel decided that it was slightly better than the one she had been using lately. She then had another look at the pizza menu. This time it was the toppings that caught her eye, rather than the prices. After staring at the shortbread for a moment, Ethel thought it would be better to wait for the taste of chocolate to satisfy her sweet tooth. She massaged her right knee briefly before standing up and making her way to the lavatory. As Ethel slid open the mirrored cupboard above the sink and lifted out Frank's bottle of Bay Rum she began to hum The Blue Danube. Then Ethel Hawkins unscrewed the cap, lifted the bottle up to her nose, inhaled the warm scent and closed her eyes.

06. COVID SHEBEEN

"Well Conor, son. It's good to see you, although it's a shame about the circumstances. Your Grandfather was a great man. This Coronavirus business is a nightmare. My auntie Agnes is in the Mater hospital now. She's been in there for weeks, but she's a fighter, not that Danny wasn't like, but you know what I mean. It's awful, so it is. Nightmare.". Conor nodded at Peter, but said nothing. He was annoyed that Peter had turned up at the funeral, as it was supposed to be close family members only due to the restrictions in place because of the Coronavirus pandemic, and Peter was only an acquaintance. He ran the local corner shop and, as far as Conor was concerned, was not to be trusted. "This is the same chapel Shane King's funeral will be in next week. Good lad he was too. Did you know Shane?", said Peter. "Aye, I went to school with him years ago. He was the only lad taller than me. Real shame that.", Conor replied. "It'll be a real shame for whoever done him in too.", Peter whispered under his breath.

Conor was exhausted. He'd been up all night at his Grandfather's wake listening to the same stories about him every time he had lifted the phone. He thought it was bizarre having a wake with hardly anyone able to visit the house. He felt awkward about having to use his Grandfather's Christian name all the time, "Danny" this, and "Danny" that. In fact everything had been strange for Conor since he had bombed The Covid Shebeen, and blown Shane King to bits in the process. He decided to brush Peter off with a joke he'd told more times in his life than any other, "My Grandfather was a staunch publican.". Peter giggled and gave Conor a pat on the back before saying, "Aye, he was a great man, son. A great man.". Conor thought about telling Peter not to touch him, as one of them could have the virus. However, he decided to keep things friendly in case Peter had connections, or was one of the boys.

Conor gazed over at the coffin and shook his head. He had always looked up to his Grandfather and this virus had given him the chance to follow in his footsteps, but there would now be no more of those steps to follow in.

In the early days of The Troubles, when many pubs in Belfast had become paramilitary targets, Conor's Grandfather had managed an illegal drinking den, or shebeen, in a house off the Grosvenor Road. He called it The Suicidal Boatman, but his patrons called it The Boat because the roofs of the houses on either side had sunk. By all accounts The Boat was a squalid affair, with a security cage inside the front door and a few threadbare sofas to sit on. However, because it was a safer alternative to nearby licensed premises, it was quite popular in its time. There had even been entertainment at the weekends provided by local musicians and singers, and the bar was dog friendly. Conor's Grandfather had once told him that the reason he'd let the dogs come in was because the house already smelled of stale urine. So, he had decided it'd be better for business if his customers thought that the stench was the fault of a Labrador, rather than a human. In 1977 a man placed a bomb outside The Boat and shouted, "You've got one minute!", through the window. It was just enough time for everyone inside to flee.

Conor had grown up listening to stories about The Boat and he wished that he could have been alive back then. Belfast seemed so dangerous and exciting during The Troubles, he thought. A lot more dangerous and exciting than managing a restaurant anyway. Conor hated his job, but it had given him enough money to start paying off a mortgage on a semi-detached house in Crumlin and buy a used Ford Focus for his daily commute to and from Belfast. A few years ago, after his wife had left him, Conor decided to turn his living room into a bar. He bought a pool table and a dartboard, but they were never really used. His Grandfather had visited a few times and stayed the night. It was a good excuse for him to see a few of his old friends who had moved out to Crumlin from West Belfast. John McCabe was one of those old friends, and Conor got to know him well. It was John that taught Conor how to make bombs. John was fond of a drink. He was so fond of a drink, in fact, that his face was now various shades of purple. He had been involved with the movement since the early 70's and would often talk with Conor into the small hours.

Conor loved listening to John's stories, but he was never sure what to believe. He'd say things like, "Did I ever tell you that Bruce Lee was one of the boys?", and Conor would laugh. "I'm telling you!", John would continue, "I was never involved in collecting protection money from local businesses. I never agreed with taking money from our community. Robbing a bank is fine, but roughing up a guy who's running an ice cream shop for a couple of hundred quid a week, and asking him how his daughter is getting on at Saint Dominic's and all of that stuff, wasn't my game. I made bombs, and I didn't even plant them either. I just made them, and I was very good at what I did. A few of them blew up our own lads in the early days and I was getting a lot of heat for that. I couldn't work it out for ages, and then it clicked with me that all of these men were married. They were all wearing their wedding rings on jobs, and the ring was completing the bloody circuit when they were arming the bombs. Once I'd figured that out we were alright.". Conor would have to get John back on track, "Aye, but what about Bruce Lee being one of the boys?".

"Oh aye, well, I was getting to that. You see, back in 1971, Paul King, Shane's late father, and big Joe Tate entered The Dragon takeaway on the Glen Road and started giving the one armed chef there a hard time. They were asking for protection money, but the Chinese guy was just off the boat and hadn't a clue what they were on about. King told me Joe threw a punch and the next thing he knew this mad chef was slicing fish gills into Joe's neck.". "McGill?!", asked Conor. "Aye, Joe entered The Dragon called Tate and walked out with the nickname McGill. That was him for life, walking around with that wild looking scarred neck on him. Obviously, Joe wanted to have the Chinaman shot for that, but Paul King was always crafty. It was Paul that talked old Bruce Lee there into letting the boys use The Dragon to enlist new recruits. Bruce never paid the boys a penny, in fact he made money off them. Once you'd been told if you joined up you'd either end up in jail, or dead, you'd be asked to order. It was a Special Fried Rice for "Yes.", or Lemon Chicken for "No.". Until old one-armed Bruce died, that was the way of The Dragon.".

Billy Best kicked with the other foot, as did his daughter Margaret, Conor's ex-wife. He had his own stories about Chinese takeaways in Ulster. "There's more Mandarin spoken in Northern Ireland than Irish, and you don't hear about that lot changing road signs. I don't like the food. I'm not interested in anything foreign, neither is anyone around here. There's a new Chinese place on the Saintfield Road with over a hundred items on the menu, and one big pot of spicy red sauce on the hob. It's a money laundering set up. No matter what you order, you'll get the same thing. Apart from the Set Meal For Two. If you order that, a hooker called Estelle arrives with a bag of Prawn Crackers and tries to steal your passport.". Margaret had often told Conor that both of their Dad's shared the same sense of humour, and that there'd be no fighting at their wedding. She'd been right about that. On the big day Danny even gave Billy a gift. "Here's a box of Israeli flags big man. You can put them up around your estate.". Billy was delighted and did just that. They were up for a fortnight before he found out they were all the flag of Honduras.

Conor set about creating The Covid Shebeen a fortnight before the country went on lockdown in order to slow the spread of Coronavirus. He bought a used Toyota Prius in Randalstown whilst wearing an N95 face mask, plastic gloves, goggles, a boiler suit and a baseball cap. The old man who sold him the motor said, "Jesus lad, you're taking this flu awful serious.". "Can't be too careful.", Conor replied, before handing over a wad of grubby cash. He then drove to the outskirts of West Belfast to meet with Sean Stokes, King of the Travellers, who made arrangements for a couple of caravans to be placed on waste ground close to the former site of The Suicidal Boatman. Then, over the coming weeks, Conor moved whatever stock he could from the restaurant he managed into those caravans. By the time lockdown was announced Conor was living in The Covid Shebeen. Back in Crumlin, the curtains in his house were drawn closed, and there was a note on his front door that read, "Sorry, no visitors due to Covid. Stay safe, Conor.". He was free to live his dream, follow in his Grandfather's footsteps, and become a staunch publican.

The first time he could recall hearing the joke about his Grandfather being a staunch publican was on a fishing trip they'd been on together in Castleblayney when Conor was a teenager. He could remember the old man's tobacco stained fingers toying with the fishing line. "If you want to catch yourself a big fish you'll need the right bait, and plenty of luck.". Conor could remember hearing those words, but he couldn't recall if they'd caught any fish that day, or any other day for that matter. He could, however, recollect asking his Grandfather why his pub had been blown up. "It was Loyalists. That's how it was in those days. They must have heard about the pub, and that was that. I can tell you this though, it was good of them to give us a minute. That was unusual. You'd never hear of that back then. I was running out the door expecting to be hit by machine gun fire. Everyone got out and up the street and then there was a crack before the building caved in on itself. I can remember people stealing things out of the rubble before the fire brigade even showed up. That was my last day being a staunch publican.".

The Covid Shebeen became a popular hang out for the local alcoholics within days of the lockdown. Conor was making money too, by charging twenty quid for a four pack of warm beer. He used the name Seamus if he was ever asked for it, but he rarely was. This was mainly due to him spending most of his time in the caravan that had a vinyl turntable inside it, along with a stack of Christy Moore albums, whilst his customers got drunk inside the other caravan, helping themselves to food from the restaurant and making a mess of the toilet floor while they were at it. Whenever he got tired he'd simply shout, "Last orders.", sell some cans, then lock the door and fall asleep to the sound of the vinyl stylus circling the end of a record. The city was quiet, aside from the noise of the occasional ambulance. Conor thought that it probably sounded much the same back when his Grandfather was running The Boat.

After a week of listening to Christy Moore records on constant rotation, Conor came to the conclusion that Unfinished Revolution was his favourite. From then on its grooves were never far from the needle.

Early on a Sunday morning Conor woke to the sound of banging on the caravan door. He shouted, "I'm a traveller. This is my home and I know my rights!", in his best attempt at a Cork accent. On previous mornings this had led to him hearing, "Hey Seamus, any chance of a drink?", or, "What time do you open?", but on this occasion he heard, "Open the door you tramp, or I'm setting fire to your Toyota.". Conor pulled on his face mask and goggles, lifted his hunting knife, and opened the door. Shane King was standing between the two caravans with a face that suggested he was having trouble counting them. "Protection money. To operate around here businesses pay protection money or else we look after them.", King said as he kicked at the ground. "I'm not a business. I'm a traveller.", Conor replied, in an accent that was now itself travelling. "You're selling cans and that's a business. So, you can give me two-hundred now, or I'm torching your motor.", King nodded towards the Prius. "I've a hundred on me. You can have that and twenty cans.", Conor said. "Alright, but it's three hundred next Sunday then.", replied King.

Around the same time as Conor watched Shane King drive away from The Covid Shebeen, alone, in an old, mud covered, Lexus, his grandfather was being loaded into an ambulance by a crew dressed for chemical warfare. Conor was informed of this a few hours later when his Mother phoned his mobile. "Your Granny said the pair of them had been feeling rough for a few days. Sweat dripping off them, and he'd been covering his food with salt and saying that he couldn't taste a thing. This morning he was struggling for air and your Granny phoned 999. She's back at her house now, self-isolating and feeling rotten. None of the family can visit either of them with all these restrictions. It's bloody madness, so it is. How are things with you?", she enquired. Conor told her that he was worried the restaurant might never open again, and that he'd been learning to bake bread by watching online tutorial videos. In reality, he couldn't care less if the restaurant went under and he hadn't baked any bread since the days when he'd been going through his divorce. Baking had taken his mind off his troubles back then, mainly because it was new to him.

Acting the part of Seamus the travelling barman was Conor's latest distraction. So, he opened up The Covid Shebeen and cranked up Unfinished Revolution. Come evening time the caravans were rocking and swaying to music, live music. A couple of lads had shown up with guitars, more than happy to play for beer, and an old woman was leading sing-songs too. She had a great voice, but her knowledge of the lyrics seemed fairly sketchy until the chorus came around. Conor got talking to her in the small hours. "I've lived here all my life. The place has always been a dump. I should have moved away across the water when I was young and had my chance. I met a lad from Glasgow at a dance hall. He was lovely and I broke his heart. That was the start of The Troubles.", she said. "I thought The Troubles started with the burning of Bombay Street.", Conor joked. "Away you! What would you know anyway? Sure, you're just a young lad yourself.", she replied, as she sat up a little on her chair. "You've a lovely voice on you. Were you in the choir at school?", Conor asked. "I've sang in shebeens, like this one, all my life.", she replied.

Conor's eyes lit up behind his goggles as the old woman continued. "Doctor Hook's, The Cracked Cup, The Sweetie Bottle, The Green Hut, The Flaming Amber, The Walking Stick and a couple around here, way back, The Sore Tooth and The Boat. That one was blown to bits one lunch time.". "Aye, I heard about that one being bombed by Loyalists and the roof falling in.", Conor said. "Loyalists my arse! That was Paul King, the greedy pig. He was forever giving the barman grief in there looking for money. Once the boys got wind of what he'd been up to they got rid of him. He had all sorts of side hustles on the go that he was keeping to himself. He'd been using the boys' guns to rob petrol stations, bars, you name it. He got a bullet through the head and his body was dumped out near Lisburn. The boys let the other side claim the hit and then buried him as another martyr to the cause. The only thing King believed in was money. Rotten man he was, and his son's just the same.". "Come and sing here this weekend, will you?", asked Conor. "I'll pop in on Saturday. My name is Minnie, and I want that up in lights!", she giggled.

Conor spent the rest of that week using his managerial skills to organise the delivery of a trailer load of Calor Gas cylinders to The Covid Shebeen. Sean Stokes had stolen them from a caravan site near Newcastle, County Down. When he delivered them to the shebeen Conor asked him to source a reliable motor for Sunday. "I'll call into your place on the Glen Road around ten in the morning. So, don't be getting too hammered on the Saturday night, right? There's a couple of grand in this for you. I'll need you to get rid of that Toyota sharpish too.". Sean poked his head into the caravan that Conor's customers had made their own. "Jesus lad, there's a wild stink of piss. Can you do three grand? I'll get you a good car sorted for Sunday, no bother at all, and I'll be quiet about it too like.". Conor agreed, "Aye, you're on. I'll give you a grand now and the rest on Sunday. Did you get me the sign I was after?". "It's in the back of the van here, you can give me a hand with it. I knocked it off down Boucher Road. Couldn't find a Mini one though. So, it's Volkswagen.", said Sean. "Christ, it'll look like I've booked The Fab Four.", Conor replied.

On Saturday morning Conor boarded a bus to Crumlin. On the way there his Mother phoned his mobile and said, "Your Grandad has been moved into intensive care. They've had him on oxygen, but he's really struggling. Granny is up the walls with the stress of it. I've told her to stop watching the news on the television. Even that idiot of a Prime Minister is in hospital with this bloody virus. You be very careful now. Keep washing your hands.". Conor assured her that he'd wash his hands and told her he loved her. When he arrived home he was happy to find the place untouched. The usual steady flow of junk mail must have stopped, and there were only a couple of bills waiting for him when he opened the front door. He made his way into the kitchen and opened the cupboard next to his washing machine. Under a pile of reusable shopping bags he located the large cake tin he was after. He placed it gently on the kitchen table, opened the lid, and looked inside. The contents looked like a marzipan covered confection, but it was Semtex. It had been a joke birthday gift from John. Conor smiled at it, then closed the lid.

When he returned to Belfast, Conor set about transforming the caravan he slept in into a large bomb packed with gas cylinders, nails, and scrap metal. Although, looking into it from outside there was no visible difference, other than the several bottles of Powers whiskey he had placed on a table by the door as he recited his grandfather's words, "If you want to catch yourself a big fish you'll need the right bait, and plenty of luck.". Conor also added a couple of steel galvanised door bolts to the outside of the caravan door and an alarm clock with a one minute timer hidden behind some breeze blocks that the caravan was mounted on. This clock was connected to the cake of Semtex. Conor was pleased with his work. "No wedding ring to worry about here, John!", he shouted into the air before laughing out loud. It was a good laugh, a proper belly laugh. Conor felt better after getting it out of his system. After that, he set to work on the other caravan. He filled it with what was left of his beer, the vinyl turntable and his Christy Moore albums. Then he propped the Volkswagen sign up next to the door.

Conor was playing Unfinished Revolution when Minnie arrived at The Covid Shebeen. "Is this my sign then?", she laughed. "Aye. Sorry it doesn't light up.", replied Conor. "Oh well, God loves a trier. What are we listening to?", asked Minnie. "Christy Moore. Unfinished Revolution. I've listened to a bunch of his albums and I think this is his best.", Conor said as he lifted the album sleeve. "Aye, that's The Goldilocks Effect. His earlier albums are quite direct and his later ones are overproduced. So, you've chosen the one in the middle, like Goldilocks in The Three Bears.", Minnie smiled. "If you think you'll be getting away with calling me Goldilocks tonight you've another thing coming!", barked Conor. "Oh, calm yourself. I can think of worse things to be calling you. Anyway, you've more pressing issues. This place reeks of urine. It reminds me of The Boat, so it does. I think the men just pissed where they stood in that place.", Minnie rolled her eyes. Conor smiled, and continued to do so late into the night. Minnie left, with a bottle of Powers whiskey under her arm, at around two in the morning, after singing Danny Boy, twice.

Shane King drove up to The Covid Shebeen shortly after dawn, parking his Lexus between the two caravans. Conor was waiting for him in the doorway next to the Volkswagen sign, dressed in his N95 face mask, plastic gloves, goggles, boiler suit and baseball cap. "Morning tinker. You know what I'm here for.", said King as he emerged from his car. "It's been a tough week. I can only give you a couple of hundred.", said Conor. "You'll be giving me your kneecaps too. I'm not playing games here!", King barked into Conor's face. "I know. Look, I've a load of whiskey in the other caravan there. How about you take that with you too. I'll sort you out with the cash in a minute.", replied Conor, pointing into the other caravan. King looked at the whiskey, then turned back to face Conor before punching him in the left ear. "Did that sting? I hate dealing with tinkers. I'm taking your whiskey, and I'll be taking your car too.", King shouted, puffing up his chest as he entered the caravan and made his way towards the bottles of Powers. Conor narrowed his eyes and slammed the caravan door shut, before locking the pair of steel galvanised door bolts.

King began kicking the inside of the door so hard that the whole caravan was shaking back and forth. Conor smiled, armed the bomb, and shouted, "You've got one minute!", before running towards his car. He slid into the driver's seat and turned the key. The Toyota started first time and Conor sped away in the direction of the Springfield Road. The bomb exploded with a deep, rumbling, sound, as flames and smoke filled the sky above the place where The Covid Shebeen had been just moments before. Conor turned on the car radio in an attempt to calm himself. The sound of It Was A Good Day by Ice Cube filled the Prius. Conor was tapping the steering wheel in time with the music when he noticed Peter carrying an empty bread crate out of his shop. Without thinking, Conor waved at Peter before realising his mistake and swerving around a corner into a side street. After a few unplanned turns Conor was back on the Springfield Road and making his way out of the city towards the Glen Road and his meeting with Sean Stokes. He was fairly confident that Peter wouldn't have recognised him behind his face mask and goggles.

When Conor arrived at the Traveller's encampment Sean Stokes was attempting, and failing, to start the engine on a black Ford Capri. "I'm sorry about this Conor. The motor was running grand yesterday. I don't know what's up with her this morning.", Sean sighed. "Right, you'll be my taxi to Crumlin then!", Conor yelled, pointing a gloved hand towards Sean's white Ford Transit. "I'm half cut lad. I've been drinking all night.", mumbled Sean. "I've two hundred quid here, on top of the rest of your money, that should get me a lift to Crumlin.", Conor complained as he adjusted his goggles, before handing Sean the cash. "Can I keep the Capri?", enquired Sean. "Aye, since it's a rusting heap. Let's go.", replied Conor. "I'll get Sharon to drive us then so. Hop in the back of the van.", Sean said, pointing towards the Transit. "This Toyota needs to disappear too lad, before we go.", Conor said as he gave Sean the keys to the Prius. "I'll get the kids over there to burn it in the back field. That'll give them something to look at, that isn't the bloody internet, for an hour, or so.", Sean rolled his eyes as he waved a couple of teenage lads over to the Toyota.

There was a handwritten note awaiting Conor when he returned home. It read, "Hi Conor. So sorry to hear about Danny. Let me know when the funeral is. John.". Conor looked at the screen on his mobile phone and realised that his battery had died. He knew that his phone could be recharged again, but he would now never be able to ask his grandfather about Paul King bombing The Boat. In fact, he wouldn't be able to talk to him about anything ever again.

Conor made his way into his kitchen and fetched a black plastic bin liner, stripped off his clothes and placed them inside it, along with his mask, gloves and goggles. After that he showered and put on his best suit. He phoned his Mother and apologised for missing all of her phone calls. He told her he had been feeling ill and had been self-isolating, but that he was now on the mend and would come through to Belfast and bring John with him. "Have you seen the news?", she asked. "No. All of this Coronavirus stuff has been too depressing. I haven't bothered with it.", he replied. "Huge fire at a Gypsy camp near The Royal this morning.", she informed him.

Conor drove to John's house in his Ford Focus, stopping off at the local Spar on the way to buy some lunch and dump his bag full of clothes into their large waste bin. John was in good form and tried his best to cheer Conor up on the way into Belfast. Conor's lack of sleep, coupled with a mild hangover, worked in his favour as he looked like he'd been ill recently, and sounded naturally upset when he spoke. When they reached his Granny's house he was fit for bed.

"Hi Conor love. Good to see you.", his Granny welcomed him with a kiss on his cheek. "Oh, sorry love, I keep forgetting not to touch people. The undertakers are holding onto your Grandad. He can't even come home.", she started to cry. "Sorry Gran. Here, I'll get the kettle on.", Conor held her shoulder. "Kettle's been on all bloody morning.", Conor's Mother appeared from the kitchen. "Glad you're here son. Jesus, you're looking rough.", she fixed his tie. "Aye, I could do with a sleep, to tell you the truth.", Conor said. "Well, go on up and have a lie down in the spare room. I'll wake you up when the dinner is ready.", she nodded.

Danny's wake was a strange affair, conducted mainly over the phone. John made sure Conor's glass was never empty. This was easy enough for him to do, as there was a steady stream of neighbours and friends leaving bottles, food and mass cards outside the front door. "That old git of a priest won't let us play Old Man River tomorrow.", complained Conor's Granny. "There'll be no one there to hear it anyway, by the sound of things.", said his Mum. "Once all of this Coronavirus business has calmed down we should have a proper family gathering in memory of Grandad.", suggested Conor. "Big Billy and Margaret are coming to the funeral. I thought that was good of them. You know what he's like coming over to this neck of the woods.", John said. "Danny was forever winding him up.", he continued. "Oh, sure, they were as bad as each other. If Billy had been born around here those two would have been as thick as thieves.", said Conor's Mum, before asking Conor how his baking skills were coming on. It took a few seconds before the penny dropped, then he said, "I can make a lemon drizzle cake now.". "Well done son.", she said.

On the morning of Danny's funeral the sun was shining and, because of the lockdown, the traffic was very light around the chapel. Outside there was birdsong and inside there was mumbling, shuffling, and the lingering smell of incense. Conor found it strange that he no longer felt any kind of emotion whenever he spoke to Margaret. It was like he couldn't even imagine ever having been attracted to her, never mind once being married to her. "How are you Conor?", she asked. "I'm a bit wreaked. I've had no sleep, what with the wake. It was good of you and Billy to come along today though. Nice to see the pair of you.", Conor did his best to smile. "I don't like funerals, but sure who does? Daddy doesn't come near West Belfast, never mind driving in with a Tricolour in the glove box!", Margaret giggled. "What?!", Conor was amazed. "Here Daddy, show Conor your flag.", Margaret tapped Billy on the shoulder. "It's not my flag, and it never will be. It's just a mark of respect Conor, so it is. Danny was a good man. Would you mind if I put this in the coffin with him son?", said Billy. "Aye, that's a nice touch. Lovely.", replied Conor.

"Cops reckon Shane blew himself up by accident, making pipe bombs in those caravans.", Peter whispered into Conor's ear. "Was he one of the boys then?", asked Conor. "Of course he was. Sure, his Da was Paul King!", Peter barked. "Aye, well, all of that doesn't mean much to me. It's a different country nowadays. Pity about Shane though, you know?", Conor sighed. "Do you know what Conor? I reckon I do know, but this isn't the time, or the place.", Peter looked Conor in the eyes. "Conor, the wee cottage in Carlingford is yours now. Your Grandad would have wanted you to have it.", Conor's Granny handed him the keys. "That's lovely. I'll get down to it soon.", said Conor. "John said he'd go down with you tonight. The pair of you can go fishing. Take your mind off things, eh?", she smiled. "Sounds good to me.", Conor replied.

"Chapels stink!", Billy said as he drove Margaret home. "I still can't believe you gave Danny an Irish flag Daddy.", said Margaret. "My hole! He's away to meet God holding a set of rosary beads in one hand and an Indian flag in the other!", Billy roared with laughter.

The cottage in Carlingford wasn't quite how Conor remembered it. The small garden was overgrown and the building itself was damp inside. "It's a tip John.", Conor shook his head. "Aye, she'll need a bit of work. It has to stay in the family though. You can't sell it. Not now anyway.", replied John. "Why is that? Can't see anyone buying it?", asked Conor. "Well, there are various reasons, but the main one I can remember is in here.", John beckoned Conor into the kitchen. Close to the back door he knelt down and peeled back the carpet. "Aye, sure there's damp everywhere.", said Conor. John lifted a floorboard, reached in, and lifted out a riffle. "Ambush at Warrenpoint, 1979. Big day for the boys. A very big day indeed.", John got to his feet. "Bloody Hell John! Did my Grandad know this was here?", Conor moved towards John to get a better look at the gun. "Well, he was a helpful sort of a man.", John smiled. "Hello? Conor, it's Peter, are you in here? We need to talk.", the voice came from the front hallway. Conor looked John in the eyes, then turned and walked towards the living room.

"Conor, there you are! I hope you don't mind me popping my head in.", Peter grinned. "Just passing, were you? Well, you might as well take a seat then.", Conor pointed to an armchair beside the fireplace. "I'll be taking more than a seat, but it'll do for starters.", Peter sat down. "Well, spit it out. What are you going on about?", asked Conor. "I know you were involved in bumping off Shane King. To be honest, I'm not personally all that bothered. It saves me a couple of hundred quid a month actually, but that's not enough. You see, I'm up to my neck in debt. Horses, slot machines, poker nights. I'd bet on the sun coming up and there'd be an eclipse.", Peter shrugged. "You're talking out of your arse Peter! Sure I've no reason to be involved in anything like that.", Conor moved to the window. "Look Conor, I'm going to make this simple. Ten grand is all I'm after. That'll get me straight. Ten grand and I'll keep my mouth shut. I know you're good for it. You've got that house in Crumlin, and now this shack as well.", Peter looked towards the kitchen door and his eyes widened in shock before John shot him in the face and chest.

"Always knew I could have been a triggerman. The boys had me on explosives because I could keep a cool head. They gave all the angry lads guns.", John lowered the riffle. Conor sat on the windowsill, "Jesus John! Christ, I wasn't expecting that.". "Neither was he!", John laughed. "I take it you've done that before then?", asked Conor. John walked towards the middle of the room, "I've a bad memory. Bad eyesight too, I could see three of him. So, I went for the one in the middle.". "Cinderella!", shouted Conor. John looked puzzled. "No, not her. What do you call the one with the porridge?", Conor asked. "Goldilocks?", John answered. "Aye, that's what she did. She went for the one in the middle.", Conor pointed at Peter's dead body. John howled, "That's a cracker!". "It's the way I tell 'em!", Conor joined in with a Frank Carson impression. John moved to the settee and sat down, resting the riffle across his knees. "Well Conor son. We'll have to take this boy's car off the road.", John nodded towards Peter. "We can throw him into the boot. Two birds, one stone.", said Conor. John smiled, "Spoken like a staunch publican.".

07. THE PLANT ROOM

You are sitting uncomfortably at your desk. You look up at the clock on the wall. It is a dirty yellow colour. It was most likely installed when people could smoke indoors. There is a layer of dust on top of the clock. The new cleaner is probably too short to reach it. She can only speak Spanish and has not completed her Health and Safety training. This is a problem and it is on your list. The old cleaner was in front of you in the queue for the till at the supermarket on Friday. You did not speak to her. She was buying a bottle of vodka and a chocolate Happy Bear Day cake that was reduced to half price because it was missing an eye. Her payment card did not work and she had to pay cash. This took a long time and it held up the whole queue. You missed your bus by thirty seconds. You are going to tell Tracey as soon as you see her. There would be no point telling George as he is on the late rota and never sees the cleaner. It is almost ten minutes past eleven. In five minutes time you will be on your fifteen minute long morning break.

You do not like Monday mornings because of the Midday Meeting. It takes place in John's office. He is a senior executive and his room is always cold. You are the most important manager. You know this because you leave every Midday Meeting with at least twice as much paperwork as Tracey and George. This is one of the reasons that you are now taking pills to lower your heart rate. The other reason is that you are not getting along well with your husband, Andy.

As you take your list out of the top drawer of your desk you can feel the sun on the back of your head. You can smell a hint of your new conditioner in the air and you can see that George is squinting with the sun in his eyes and trying to hide from it in your shadow. You consider making a joke about him winking at you, but you decide not to. He was a bit strange at the office Christmas party and he has stopped talking about his girlfriend. You place your list on your desk and begin to read over it. You are happy that all of the major tasks from last week have been completed and are now scribbled out. You look up at the clock on the wall again.

It is eleven minutes past eleven. You think about time and how it seems to slow down whenever you want it to speed up. Your lower back hurts and you need to stand up and stretch. You decide you will go to the toilet before your morning break begins as time goes too quickly whenever you are on your break. You stand up. Your head feels slightly dizzy as you listen to George complain that there should be window shades in the office. You tell him that you think it is a good idea and that he should bring it up with John at the Midday Meeting. You watch as George makes a note on his list and then you walk out of the office.

Tracey is standing in the corridor with her left index finger in her ear. She is holding her phone against the right side of her head and looking at the floor. You can smell cigarette smoke, coffee and hairspray. The florescent tube outside John's office has blown and you hope that Tracey has put it on her list because she would have seen it first. You wonder if she is looking at the floor to avoid the florescent tube job. You think it is the sort of thing she would do.

You make your way to the manager's toilets. You are glad that you no longer have to use the staff toilets on the factory floor. There are two cubicles for you to choose from. You enter the one on the left as it has the strongest flush. There is no graffiti on the back of the door of the cubicle and, although there are two toilets in the room, you always seem to have the manager's toilets to yourself. While you urinate you think about the time you were in the staff toilets and the old cleaner was in the cubicle next to yours. You recall her loud farts and grunts and how the smell made you gag. It was so bad that tears ran down your cheeks and ruined your smokey eye make-up. Tracey said you looked like a sad panda bear that day. You did not find her remark funny at the time, but you think it is funny now, looking back. There is good quality toilet paper for you to use and the sound of the powerful flush reassures you. You wish your toilet at home had a powerful flush too. Andy pretended to gag this morning as he brushed his teeth after you had been to the lavatory. You are sad and angry when you are at home. You wash your hands.

You look at your face in the mirror while you dry your hands with a paper towel. You are Joanna Jenkins. You are thirty years old and you think you look stern. You scan your black bob haircut. There are no wiry grey strands for you to pluck today. Your face is thin and your nose is pointed. It reminds you of your aunt Carol's nose. You do not like your aunt Carol or her nose. You did not look stern when you worked on the factory floor. You have a manager's face now. It is a face that does not wish to be asked stupid questions. A face that is too busy to stop and chat. You wonder if your smokey eye make-up is still in fashion. You decide that if it is no longer trendy you are going to stick with it anyway. You have perfected the look now and you don't have the time, or the money, to spend on anything new. Your lips are thin and dry. You suspect that if you leave Andy you will struggle to attract another handsome man. You think about the way George looked at you at the office Christmas party. You no longer wish to look at your face and your hands are now dry. You throw the used paper towel into the bin and make your way to the canteen.

The factory canteen serves very basic food and drink. You are comfortable eating here. The factory staff leave the table by the window free for the managers and that is where you are now sitting. You think your bacon roll tastes overly salty today and there is not enough ketchup in it for your liking. You prefer the sweet taste of your orange juice, but you feel the glass is too small. It reminds you of the time Andy took you to a fancy hotel in the city centre and you ordered a Japanese beer. The snooty barman remarked that the beer was actually brewed here in Edinburgh and Andy laughed. It is that sort of behaviour that you feel is destroying your marriage. Andy seems to think there are no problems between you, but you know that there are and you are not going to tell him. If he really loved you he would know. Your favourite times at home now are when Andy is not there. Last night you watched a train leaving Waverley Station from North Bridge and you wished you were leaving too. You feel like you want to cry. You need to think about something else. You finish your orange juice and leave most of your bacon roll uneaten.

The clock in the canteen is digital. It is eleven forty-two. Your fifteen minute long morning break ended twelve minutes ago. You do not care. The soles of your feet feel too hot. You take off your shoes and gaze at the digital clock on the wall. You decide that when the time is eleven forty-five you will put your shoes back on and go to The Plant Room for ten minutes. After that you will go to the Midday Meeting. You start to consider that this might be your favourite part of the working week. Your list is almost empty. That is as good as it gets in this place. You know that once the Midday Meeting is over you will have a new list of tasks to complete and none of them will yet be finished and scribbled out. You wish your life was different. You never dreamed of being a manager in a factory. You do not think that anyone, anywhere, ever dreamed of being a manager in a factory. You cannot think of a good way out of your situation. Your lower back is still sore and your tummy does not feel good. You pass wind and you decide that you need to put your shoes back on and leave the canteen quickly even though it is only eleven forty-four.

The Plant Room is dusty and filled with equipment. You know that some of the machines are part of the air conditioning system for the building as you had to find this room with a workman last month after John complained that his room was not cold enough. You have visited The Plant Room several times since then to do stretches that help ease your back pain and to cry. You have decided that if you are ever discovered stretching in The Plant Room you will explain that you heard a loud grinding noise and you are investigating it. You have not yet decided what you will do if you are discovered crying in The Plant Room.

You make your way to the far corner of The Plant Room and place a hand on each wall before you look up at the ceiling. You move your feet back a step and then you lean towards the corner. Your arms take the weight of your upper body and your lower back pain eases greatly. You move your right foot further back from the corner before bending your left knee. The stretching feeling in your right calf makes you incredibly happy and you hold this position for thirty seconds.

You move your right foot towards the wall before sliding your left foot back and bending your right knee. The stretching feeling in your left calf is not very satisfactory and you only hold this position for twelve seconds. You begin to walk slowly around The Plant Room. You think the equipment looks very old and outdated, but you are not sure what any of it does. You notice the crumpled wrapper of a chocolate bar on the floor beside a large machine that is making a quiet rumbling sound. You are alarmed at the sight of this litter as it was not there the last time you were in The Plant Room. You are upset that someone else has found this space and is using it to relax in. You wonder if the person who ate the chocolate bar had thought of a good excuse to use had they been discovered in The Plant Room. You are now worried that someone might see you leaving The Plant Room and find the chocolate wrapper. You kick the chocolate wrapper underneath the large machine. You are concerned that you are breathing too quickly. It is time for you to take one of your heart slowing pills. Your clothes are soaked with a layer of cold sweat.

There is a rattling sound coming from some pipes near the door of The Plant Room. You feel unsafe and quickly make your way to the door. You take a long and slow breath. You can feel your heart beating in your ears. You hope that your face looks stern as you exit The Plant Room and make your way back to the office. The dirty yellow coloured clock on the office wall informs you that the Midday Meeting will begin in three minutes. You are the only person in the office. This means that Tracey and George are likely already in John's office. You do not care. You take your list out of the top drawer of your desk, along with a notebook and two pens. You always bring two pens to the Midday Meeting so that if one pen runs out of ink you will have another to hand. Tracey has asked to borrow your extra pen during two previous Midday Meetings. You are sure that you are the most important manager because of the extra pens and paperwork that you deal with. You put one of your heart slowing pills into your mouth and swallow it with the aid of some saliva. You do not have time for water as you need to go to John's office immediately.

John's office feels even colder than it usually does because you are soaked in sweat. Tracey nods a greeting at you because John is already talking and filling the air with business speak. You hate corporate jargon. John explains that he has been running the numbers and wants to hit the ground running with the new corporate strategy. You sit down and tell him that, although your plate is full, you are all over it and are looking forward to getting the ball rolling with this before close of play. John looks at George and explains that we will need all hands on deck. George asks John if we can have window shades in the office and explains that you think it is a good idea. John looks at you with an angry expression and tells you that you know that there is no budget for this. You nod and think about stabbing John in his left eye with your extra pen. You want to scream in George's creepy little face. John asks you if the new cleaner has completed her Health and Safety training. You inform John that it is on your list. John advises you to keep your eye on the ball. You nod and think about stabbing John in his right eye with your extra pen.

You begin a new list with the word cleaner. You ask Tracey if she has florescent tube on her list. Tracey does not know what you mean. You ask Tracey if she has the light bulb outside John's office on her list. Tracey informs you that she did not know that the light bulb outside John's office needed to be on a list. You add the words florescent tube to your new list. Your lips are now contracted and feel numb. You are certain that you look very stern. You tell Tracey that you missed your bus because the old cleaner was buying vodka. Tracey explains to the room that she thinks that you discussing the old cleaner at the Midday Meeting is very inappropriate. John informs you that your behaviour is not best practice and that he may need to touch base with you about this going forward. You protest to George that you have been thrown under a bus. George asks you not to move the goalposts on this. Tracey tells you it is what it is. John angrily explains that if he cannot get all of his ducks in a row we will be back to the drawing board. You apologise to the room. You scribble the word avenge on your new list. Your body feels very tense.

You leave the Midday Meeting with a large amount of paperwork, a new list of jobs to complete and a headache. The pain is behind your eyes and across your forehead. It reminds you of the headaches you suffered as a child whenever you ate ice cream too quickly. You want to cry or be violent. You are very sad and angry whenever you are at work.

You place the paperwork from the Midday Meeting on top of your desk and slide your new list into the top drawer. You now have enough work to ensure that you will not have time to talk to George or Tracey until you have devised a plan to destroy them. You think that George will be easy to trip up and that Tracey only needs to be given enough rope. You smile in an angry way as you look up at the dirty yellow coloured clock on the wall. It is time for lunch. You hear your mobile phone beep. It is a message from Andy apologising for upsetting you. He would like to treat you to a meal right now. He has booked a table at your favourite Italian restaurant. You like the three cheese pizza there. You are smiling in a happy way. You are crying.

08. HOW I GOT MY SCAR

Dave opened his eyes as wide as he could and searched for the thin crack on his bedroom ceiling that began at his light fixture. He then attempted to stop his head from nodding rhythmically back and forth by gently turning it to the right and looking towards the window. The amber glow of a street light was making a rippling effect along the top of the curtains as he forced the side of his face into the pillow and tried to recall the names of all six of his primary school teachers.
Gemma alternated the movements of her right hand as she encircled the base of Dave's manhood. Most of the time her lips and hand moved in unison up and down the length of his shaft, but occasionally they worked against each other. Gemma did this in order to remove the odd stray pubic hair from her mouth, but she hoped that Dave thought it was an exciting technique. After a slow upward lick along his tool she lifted her head, removed a hair tie from her left wrist and tied her long, blonde, mane into a ponytail as she grinned at Dave.

Mister Swan had taught Dave during his forth year in primary school. He must have been close to retirement age back then and he was probably dead now. Dave tried to recall the heavy must of Mister Swan's notorious body odour, and the way that a cream coloured build up of saliva used to sway about on the middle of the old man's bottom lip. Bobby Grant had once told Dave that Mister Swan walked around his classroom barefoot on hot days. Dave tried to visualise that, but he couldn't get a clear image, then his mind drifted towards thinking about what Bobby might be up to these days.

Gemma squeezed Dave's penis firmly with her left hand, then gently spanked each of his testicles with the tips of the fingers on her free hand. She giggled as she watched them contract towards his body. Her eyes widened as she had an idea. Gemma crawled up the bed and placed her body between Dave's face and the light above the curtains that he had been gazing at. She slowly took off her bra before letting her hair down again and shaking her head. Gemma then formed her hair tie into a figure of eight in front of Dave's eyes.

Bobby Grant had been a year ahead of Dave the whole way through school. Dave pondered how things like that had seemed so important when he was young, and how they held no sway now as he looked up at Gemma's tits. He had never seen them before. Well, he had seen tits before, he just hadn't seen Gemma's. He had felt them though. Last night, just before she had bitten his bottom lip. He thought they had felt round and heavy, but his mind was changing now. Maybe they were pointy, or pert? Dave's eyebrows moved closer together as he wondered if pointy and pert were real words. Then his thoughts turned to Gemma's hair tie and why she was playing about with it in front of his eyes.

Gemma slipped her hair tie over Dave's cock and twisted it at the base. She then stretched the lower circle of the figure of eight over his balls and released her fingers, cupping her right hand over his nuts as they tightened. As Gemma felt Dave's warm hand running up the back of her left thigh she wondered if she needed to pee, if she was better than Dave's last girlfriend and if every young man lived in a video game strewn dump.

Dave's eyes shut tight, his left hand grasped the side of the mattress and something deep within his belly tightened until he felt queasy. Gemma had apologised for biting his lip the night before and told him it had been an accident, but now that his balls were in some sort of a knot Dave was beginning to have doubts. He tried to calm himself by thinking that maybe this was what everyone got up to these days. In the five years he had been with Sharon a lot of things could have changed in the World of sex, especially now that people could find out about it all online. This was probably normal, and that worried him. He took a deep breath and decided that, whatever the topping, a pizza is still a pizza. He wasn't entirely sure what that meant, but as he slowly moved his right hand over the underside of Gemma's knickers he noticed that they were wet and warm. Dave wondered if there was money to be made in reminding people that, whatever the topping, a pizza is still a pizza. As he felt Gemma's mouth enveloping his dick again he tried to think of what age Bobby would be now. Probably still just a year older, more or less.

Gemma wondered if things were moving too fast with Dave. Then she worried that he might think her bum looked big in the dark and if she had chosen knickers that looked sexy from behind. When her mind began to tell her that a cheese pizza would be great right about now, Gemma decided that she should really focus on the job in hand. Perineal massage was to be tonight's chef's special. Gemma had heard all about it from her friend Audrey. So, after a short time kneading Dave's balls like dough until his left knee shot up towards the stars, she began to massage bellow his gonads, in search of the little lump that Audrey had told her about. As Dave slipped his fingers into Gemma's pants he reminded himself to always be a gentleman, and that ladies should come first. Although, he was struggling with this, as no matter how hard he tried to think about a repulsive, and probably dead, teacher, or the age difference between him and an old friend, his toes wanted to stretch out and his body wanted to shoot the contents of his balls into orbit. His fingers found Gemma's clitoris and vibrated like an electric toothbrush.

Gemma arched her lower spine and threw her head back. As she looked up she noticed something on the ceiling near the light fixture and hoped that it wasn't a spider web. She decided that she would invite Dave to her place next time. As her fingers located the little lump that Audrey had told her about, Gemma gently rocked her body up, down and along Dave's fingers. Then she began to match the speed of his vibration as the fingers of her right hand rubbed his little lump and her left hand gently stroked his prick.

Dave was now fairly certain that he would need to readjust to life as a blind man and that his eyes would likely never open again. The back of his right hand was dripping wet and Gemma's body was thrusting towards his fingers harder, and for longer, each time. Dave tried to slowly count his lower teeth with his tongue, as his eyelids began to bubble and his ears filled with white noise. Gemma made a short, pained, noise and lowered herself onto Dave's fingers as he stretched out his entire body and exploded from somewhere deep within. Their bodies shuddered and rolled towards each other.

After several slow, deep, breaths Dave guided Gemma into his arms and said, "I haven't felt that good since Leigh Griffiths scored two free kicks against England in 2017.". Gemma laughed and then replied, "Didn't that match end in a draw?". Dave smiled, "I think our match ended in a draw and all.". Gemma ran her hands along his chest, up his neck and onto his face before she kissed him softly and slowly. The amber light making its way into the room from around the curtains was gradually being replaced with daylight. Gemma gazed at Dave's face, then gently ran an index finger along the mark on his forehead. "I need to go to the loo. When I get back you can tell me what happened to your face, if you want.", Gemma said as she rolled over to get out of bed. "Oh, I can. Can I?", replied Dave, "Lucky me, I can't wait. Alright, I'll tell you, but you're getting us both a glass of water while I'm in the loo.". Dave bounded out of bed and ran in the direction of the bathroom. Gemma threw his pillow after him and shouted, "You're a wanker! Absolute prick!". "Aye, mind and get the water.", Dave replied from inside the bathroom.

Gemma switched the bedside lamp on before scanning the floor in search of Dave's hoodie. She located it under her jeans and socks, which she kicked out of the way as she stood up. The hoodie felt heavier than Gemma had expected it to as she lifted it up from the floor. She pulled it over her head and rolled up the sleeves before smoothing the cotton over her thighs. When she had finished adjusting the garment the hem rested just above her knees. Gemma fingered the muff of Dave's hoodie in search of its opening before deciding that it hung too low for her to comfortably slide her hand into. She made her way to the kitchen and turned on the cold tap to let it run whilst she searched for a pair of pint glasses. Dave appeared in the doorway and smiled at Gemma. "My hoodie looks better on you than it does on me! Here, I'll sort out the water. The loo's free now.", he said, as he made his way towards the cupboard above the toaster that he kept his glasses in. "I knew they'd be in the one cupboard I didn't try.", Gemma grumbled, as she dashed off to the bathroom. "Aye, that's always the way.", Dave replied.

Once back in the bedroom, Dave did his best to tidy the place up. He collected all of the scattered clothing from the floor and placed it on a chair. Then he made the bed, arranging the pillows so that he and Gemma would be able to sit up and talk for a while. He climbed onto the bed and made himself comfortable before taking a large gulp from his glass of water. Dave heard the toilet flush and attempted to arrange his body into a shape he thought might look attractive. He soon decided that he had no idea what arrangement of limbs might look better than any other and resolved to simply hold his belly in as best he could as Gemma walked into the room. "Do you mind if I skin up?", Gemma asked as she reached for the wooden box on Dave's bookshelf. "Sure, go ahead.", Dave answered, letting his stomach rise to wherever it wanted to be. "I'm going to toast the tobacco. I read about it in a book that my Brother had all about different kinds of weed.", Gemma said as she lifted two cigarettes and a lighter from inside the box. She continued, "I think I just need to run a flame along the cigs without them catching fire.". "Cool.", said Dave.

Gemma sat down at the foot of the bed and placed the wooden box by her side. Dave watched as she toasted the tobacco, then said, "There's a rolling mat in the box if you want to use it. I can't actually roll. Well, I can, but they end up too tight.". Gemma pulled out the rolling mat and placed it on her knees. Dave moved down the bed and lifted a pack of rolling papers from inside the box. He removed three from the pack. "I hate the taste of glue!", he exclaimed as he joined them together, before placing his handiwork onto the rolling mat. He then ripped off a strip of cardboard from the packet of papers ahead of throwing them back into the box. "I can roll a roach with one hand though.", he joked. Gemma smiled as Dave placed the roach onto the rolling mat. He moved forward slightly and tucked some of Gemma's hair behind her ear with his right hand, then he kissed her before moving back up the bed and making himself comfortable. "So, are you going to tell me how you got your scar?", Gemma asked, smiling and raising her eyebrows. Dave lowered his eyes, took a deep breath, and said, "Aye, I'll tell you.".

"My Mum came from a large family. I think there were eight kids, or something like that.", Dave began. "You mean you don't know how many Aunts and Uncles you have?", asked Gemma. Dave laughed, "Well, I'm not really close to my family, and they're scattered all over the place now. I just know that my Mum was the youngest of the real ones, and then there was Kenny who was adopted. He was always in trouble. I wouldn't be surprised if he was in jail now, or dead even.". "Oh, that's kind of sad. It sounds like a complicated family anyway.", Gemma said. She created a little valley in the middle of the rolling mat and arranged the the paper and roach before asking, "Mind if I mix and match?". Dave replied, "Yes, no worries. The grass is good, but the solid is just Soap Bar.". Gemma lit a lighter and held it under one end of a small piece of hash until it began to burn slightly. She then crumbled it along the length of the paper in the rolling mat. After placing the hash back into the wooden box she picked up a small bag of weed and opened it. "Smells strong enough anyway.", she commented as she tore at the contents.

"Is there not a grinder in there Gemma?", Dave pointed towards the box. "Oh, aye, I can see it now. It must have been under the bag.", she answered. Gemma opened the grinder and placed a couple of buds and a few leaves inside. Once she had ground it all to a fine powder she tipped the contents of the grinder into the palm of her left hand before flaking it on top of the hash. "Getting there!", she asserted. "Right, so, what have your family got to do with your scar then?", Gemma asked, as she began to crumble the toasted tobacco out from inside the scorched cigarettes along the length of the centre of the rolling mat. Dave scratched his head, stretched out his legs and said, "Well, when I was a kid, I think I was four years old, maybe five, Kenny had to babysit me one night while my Mum was out with the ones from her work.". "What did your Mum do? For work, I mean.", asked Gemma. "Office stuff. I don't really know.", Dave replied. Gemma cradled the underside of the mat, rolled it back and forth, licked along the length of the paper and rolled the mat a final time before lifting out the long spliff.

Dave admired Gemma's craftsmanship by nodding his approval as he gazed at the joint in her hand, then said, "Kenny had been in some sort of young offenders centre for a while and he had made a couple of ashtrays for my Mum, and a really long poker for our fire. Mum told me she didn't like the poker because it didn't match the little shovel and brush that she had. The poker was about twice the length of my Mum's shovel. The bloody thing looked like a metal walking stick! It was just daft.". Gemma giggled as she put everything back into the wooden box as neatly as she could in order to close the lid. She put the spliff into her mouth, wiped away some stray tobacco from Dave's hoodie, then stood up and made her way to the bookshelf with the box. "Oh, you've got Playpower by Richard Neville! My Dad gave that to my Brother ages ago. It's like The Rough Guide To Getting Stoned.", Gemma laughed as she returned the wooden box to the shelf it had been on, before turning towards Dave and lighting the joint. "Yes, that's an old Hippie book. Bit of a classic. Although, it would probably just be a blog if it was written today.", Dave quipped.

Gemma lifted an ashtray that was balancing on top of a stack of vinyl singles. "Is this one of Kenny's?", she asked. "No. I've no idea where his ashtrays ended up. Probably in a landfill site now.", Dave answered as Gemma made her way towards the bed. She took a long draw on the spliff and held the smoke in her lungs, then she handed it to Dave and crawled over the bed sliding the ashtray along the duvet in front of her. "Smooth landing.", said Dave. He tapped the bed twice beside his bum, ushering Gemma towards him, before smoking the joint. Gemma giggled and then coughed as the smoke rushed out of her body. "Here.", said Dave, as he handed her his glass of water. Gemma nodded her approval then took several small drinks. "Actually, that one was mine. Doesn't matter really. There's another glass here whenever you need it.", Dave pointed towards his bedside table as Gemma edged up the bed and grasped the top of his arm. "Thanks. Perfect timing there with the water.", she said, smiling and looking up at his face. Dave transferred the spliff to his left hand then put his right arm around Gemma.

"Anyway, that night when Kenny was babysitting me. Well, I wasn't a baby, but you know what I mean. I remember waking up in bed and feeling really cold. My Mum would always have left the hall light on and my bedroom door open a bit, but it was pitch-black. After a couple of minutes I could sort of see things. You know the way your eyes get adjusted to the dark?", Dave asked. Gemma nodded and reached for the spliff. Dave took a long draw, held the smoke in his lungs, then handed it to her. He tilted his head back lazily until it rested against the headboard. Then he exhaled slowly and continued, "I got out of bed. I can only remember wearing a long white t-shirt now, but I'm sure I would have had pants on, or shorts. I can't remember. I just know that my legs and arms were cold. The room was freezing. When I opened my bedroom door I could hear voices down in the living room. I didn't know what time it was. I just guessed that my Mum was back from her night out. So, I started to make my way down the stairs. That's when I saw that the front door was wide open.". Gemma's eyes darted towards Dave's face.

"What? Am I freaking you out?", Dave asked. Gemma opened her eyes wide and said, "A bit.". "Well, you did ask me how I got my scar. I haven't even got to the scary bit yet about the guy with the knife.", Dave smiled. Gemma bounced forward, "You are kidding me?!" she asked. "Aye, I'm only messing.", Dave replied. "Wanker!", Gemma said as she slapped his chest. "It was a woman with a knife.", Dave laughed. Gemma laughed too, before settling back and taking a smoke. Dave moved his right hand upwards until he found the side of Gemma's head, then he ran his fingers back and forth through her hair at her temple. "So, I could hear someone talking in the living room, but it wasn't my Mum, or even Kenny.", Dave paused as he felt Gemma tapping his belly with the underside of the glass. He returned what was left of the water to his bedside table before Gemma passed the joint to him. Dave took a quick smoke and breathed out through his nose. He held the spliff in front of his face while he tried to remember where he was in his story. Then he nodded, took a longer draw and flicked some ash into the ashtray.

"We had a phone table back then. That's the way it was when everyone just had a landline out in the hall. Our table had a seat on it and a drawer underneath the phone. So, I walked down the last few stairs. Well, I probably swung over the third one from the bottom because it used to creak. It sounds like I was acting all cool, but I remember being dead scared passing the front door. So, I ran to get the phone book out of the drawer and then I wedged the front door closed with it.", Dave stopped in order to take a draw from the spliff before he passed it to Gemma. "Why didn't you just close the door properly? Was that because you didn't want anyone to hear you?", Gemma asked as she lifted the joint to her lips. "The door was on the latch and I don't think I could reach up. Maybe I didn't know how to work the lock? This is all a long time ago. I can remember sitting on the seat of the phone table. There was hardly any padding on that thing. So, you'd end up with a dead arse if you sat there too long.", Dave smiled at Gemma, who giggled as she blew smoke out of her mouth. "A dead arse? That's funny.", she smiled.

Dave grinned, rubbed his left eye with the palm of his hand, and continued, "So, I'm sitting on the phone table, with my wee legs swinging about, and I can see into the front room. The living room door wasn't properly open, just a few inches, but if I moved my head around I could see in and Kenny was sitting in my Mum's chair. There were a few of his crazy mates lying about the floor drinking from bottles of cider, smoking cigs, and listening to this one lad who was pacing about in front of the fire. Now, these were Kenny's mates. So, we're talking about joyriders and burglars here, and I'm sitting in the dark and the house is freezing. I didn't want to go into the front room though because of Kenny's pals, and I didn't want to go back up the stairs to bed. I guess I was just hoping my Mum would arrive back. Anyway, I was close enough to hear what the wee guy marching about in front of the fire was saying. He was hyper and a bit emotional, talking about his dead Grandfather.". Gemma took a final hit from the joint and passed it back to Dave. She then turned her body towards his and cuddled into him, resting her head upon his chest.

Dave held the spliff between the thumb and forefinger of his left hand and brought it up to his mouth. After inhaling several times in short, sharp, bursts he said, "Burned my lip. Knew it.", then he stubbed out the joint and placed the ashtray on bedside table. "Sorry about your lip babe. That was a total accident last night.", Gemma said as she rubbed Dave's belly. "Oh, I know that. No worries. I would have burned my lip anyway on the arse end of that spliff with the heat of it.", Dave lifted the full glass of water to his face and took several gulps, then he asked Gemma, "Do you want some?". "No thanks. My throat's alright now.", she replied. Dave returned the glass to the bedside table and said, "Oh, I'd say your throat is more than alright.". "Not funny!", stated Gemma as she poked a finger into his stomach. "Hey! Alright, alright, fair enough.", Dave turned around to face Gemma, smiled broadly, then moved forward and kissed her forehead. "Well, are we friends again?", he asked. "Friends? Is that what we are?", Gemma inquired, narrowing her eyes, then she grinned and continued, "Right, get on with your story.".

Dave looked down at his chest before moving his left hand towards Gemma's right. As their fingers interlocked he asked, "Where was I?". "Well, as far as I can remember, you could hear a friend of Kenny's talking about his dead Grandad, and you were also worried about your own dead arse.", Gemma laughed. "Oh, yes. Cool. Right, so I could hear this guy and he was sort of emotional, but his mates weren't taking the piss out of him for it. They were all just quiet and listening. He was saying that his Grandfather had died that week and the funeral hadn't happened yet. Then he was going on about how great his Grandad was, taking him and his wee Brother to Celtic Park, Old Firm games and all this stuff. Then he said something mad, and even these hard lads, well, you could tell they were freaked out. He said, 'Last night I woke up and I saw him standing over my wee Brother's bed! My wee Brother was fast asleep, and you know how we've been sharing a room since my Sister broke up with that prick? So, I'm in the bed by the door, it's freezing cold and I'm looking over and my Grandfather is leaning against the wall, glowing!' ".

Dave could feel Gemma's fingers loosening around his own, so he squeezed them tighter with his left hand as his right hand rubbed the top of her head. He continued, "So, I'm pretty much frozen to the seat on the phone table then. I'm not just physically cold, but I don't feel like I can actually move. The lads in the living room are all dead silent and this guy starts explaining, 'The bed I'm in is by the door. The door is closed. The light's off and my Grandad is glowing, and he's leaning against the wall. He's looking down at my wee Brother who's asleep. His bed was glowing too, or it was lit up with the glow off our Grandfather, or something. That's all bright, blinding, but my bed and the rest of the room is in darkness, pitch-black. I was looking at my Grandfather's hand pushing against the wall beside this Celtic poster we have up, and it looks like it's burning, melting! Then my Grandfather turns around and looks right at me, and that's all I can remember. I must have been knocked out, or something. So, I woke up this morning and I'm thinking it's just a dream, a nightmare, but then I looked at the wall and there's a handprint scorched into it!' ".

Gemma lurched forward and stared back at Dave, who went on, "Right then the front door flew open and I jumped up off the phone table and ran into the living room, and that's all I can remember.". "What do you mean?", asked Gemma. Dave sat up, "Well, from what my Mum told me, all Hell broke loose! She said she came in from her night out and nearly tripped over the phone book. Then, when she looked up, I was lying on the floor outside the living room with my white t-shirt covered in blood.". "Oh my God! What the Hell happened to you?", Gemma gasped. Dave looked down towards his knees, "Kenny told my Mum that he had put me to bed before his friends called in to the house. He said they were having a few drinks and one of them was telling a scary story. Then I flew into the room like a ghost and someone threw the big poker at me!". "Oh Dave! That's absolutely crazy. Who threw the poker?", Gemma ran her hand along Dave's forehead. He looked into Gemma's eyes, "My Mum thinks it was Kenny, but he said he didn't know who it was because it all happened so fast. Anyway, that's how I got my scar.".

09. FREYA LOVES GRACE

Shortly after midday on a hot, late August, afternoon Freya Miller made her way along a path beside the River Tay, near Dunkeld. She passed by the Birnam Oak, a tree made famous by William Shakespeare, and came to a stop a couple of minutes later on a small beach. Freya was dressed in black. Her Mother didn't like the colour and once told Freya, "Black will make you sweat. It absorbs sunlight.". Freya had responded, "Then why does it look so cool?", but she never received an answer. Even Freya's fingernails were painted black. She noticed that some of the polish had chipped off the nail on her right index finger when she bent down to unzip her backpack before emptying its contents onto the sand. A large can of energy drink, two bars of chocolate, a hammer, a flat-head screwdriver and a couple of metres of blue rope lay in front of her on the beach. Freya picked up the hammer and screwdriver and made her way to the foot of the tree her best friend Grace had hung herself from the previous Summer.

Some of the roots of the tree were large enough for her to balance her feet on. Although, by the time she had carved the letter F into its trunk she had slipped twice and her left ankle felt sprained and almost as sore as her right arm was from hammering. The smell of the wood reminded Freya of the technology department at her school. Grace used to sit beside her when they had a woodwork class together. A girl called Eve had tried to take Grace's seat at the start of this year and Freya had shouted "Fuck off!" at her. The teacher, Mr Brown, asked Eve to find another seat and tucked Grace's stool under the workbench.

An elderly couple walked by with a Yorkshire Terrier on a lead. The old man pointed at Freya as she was hammering and said "Disgraceful!", but she didn't stop. In fact, Freya only paused whenever she felt the sensation of pins and needles in her left hand and decided to shake the screwdriver by her side for a few seconds. By the time she had carved her name, FREYA, into the trunk of the tree the pensioners were long gone and Alfie Burns had joined her on the beach.

Alfie was ten years old, four years younger than Freya, and liked football and watching gamers streaming online. "I've done that for COYS on a tree in the Beatrix Potter Garden.", said Alfie, pointing at the lettering Freya had carved into the tree. "Who's Coys?", asked Freya. "It means Come On You Saints. Saints are St. Johnstone.", Alfie answered as he eyed up the chocolate bars on the beach. "They'll be all melted.", he said as he picked one of them up. "It's squidgy.", he remarked as he bent the bar out of shape. Freya looked at Alfie's face before her eyes darted down to the chocolate in his hand. "Well, you've melted it now, haven't you?", she asked, whilst pointing her screwdriver at him. "Can I have it then?", Alfie enquired. Freya walked over to her scattered belongings and picked up her can of energy drink before answering him, "Yes, you can have it, you prick.". Alfie smiled and said, "Thanks.". Freya opened the can and gulped long and hard on its contents before burping in Alfie's face. Alfie laughed and said, "You stink, and you're all sweaty.". "Shut up! It's because I'm wearing black and it's roasting, you moron!", Freya retorted.

Freya drank some more of her energy drink as she gazed at her handiwork. Then she turned to Alfie and asked, "Did you write COYS as big as my FREYA?". Alfie squinted his eyes at the tree as he thought about her question. "I think so. The letters weren't as fat, but they were probably the same size.", he answered. "My arms are getting tired, but I need to write two more words. If you do the middle one for me you can have that other bar of chocolate.", Freya pointed towards the warped candy wrapper on the sand. "It's melted.", Alfie stated. "So is the one in your face!", Freya barked. Alfie looked at the tree before asking, "What's the word?". "LOVES is the word.", Freya replied. Alfie was puzzled and enquired, "Loves who?". "FREYA LOVES GRACE. There's five letters in each word and they sit on top of each other. Well, LOVES is under FREYA. That's the one you're doing.", Freya said as she handed Alfie her carving tools. "I'm not doing LOVES, that's stupid!", Alfie laughed. "It's not stupid Alfie. It's what grown ups write on trees. COYS is for babies.", Freya looked him in the eyes. "Alright.", said Alfie, "I'll do LOVES.".

While Alfie was busy carving LOVES into the trunk of the tree Freya played with the rope and gazed at the branches hanging over the beach. "Tell me if you see anyone coming!", Alfie shouted over his shoulder. "There's no one here. Anyway, you're with me so you'll be fine.", Freya answered as she looped the rope between her hands before tossing it onto the sand. She turned and looked at the river. The Tay was dark and swirling. Freya kicked off her trainers and stepped into the water. She liked how the sudden drop in temperature seemed to make her sore ankle feel better. The bottom of her black jeggings were now soaked, but Freya didn't mind. After a couple of minutes she walked back onto the beach and sat down on the sand. She watched some flies hovering above the river and listened to the sound of Alfie's hammering until, eventually, he said, "Finished!". Freya wiped the sand off her feet, as best she could, put her trainers on, and stood up. Alfie handed her the hammer and screwdriver and asked, "Why did Grace die?". Freya walked towards the tree and answered, "Because of her Uncle.".

Alfie lifted the second, melted, chocolate bar. It felt floppy in his hand. "This one is chocolate juice.", he said. "Chocolate milkshake, Alfie. There's no such thing as chocolate juice.", said Freya as she surveyed Alfie's carving. "You did a good job. Your LOVES is the right size.", she remarked, as she moved to steady her feet on top of the roots again. "When I grow up I'm going to invent chocolate juice and be a millionaire.", said Alfie as he slowly opened the packaging. "Everyone will like chocolate juice.", he continued, as melted chocolate began to dribble through his fingers. The pins and needles returned to Freya's left hand. "Alright, Alfie, you can invent chocolate juice when you're older.". Alfie squeezed the runny chocolate into his mouth before making his way to the river to wash his hands. "I'm not putting my feet in.", said Alfie. "You don't have to.", replied Freya, who was busy making sure the letters of GRACE were directly under the letters of LOVES. It seemed to take less time to carve the last word. When she'd finished Freya was happy with her work. She turned towards Alfie and noticed the rope in the water.

"Alfie! What the fuck are you doing?", Freya screamed. Alfie turned around, shocked, and replied, "Fishing. I'm fishing for fish.". "The rope is wet now, you dick! I don't want wet rope. Grace didn't have a fucking wet rope!", Freya shouted as she bounded onto the beach. "I'm sorry.", said Alfie, "I was bored.". "Fuck sake, Alfie.", she exhaled. Freya looked out into the river and watched the rope snaking around. "Why won't it sink?", she asked. "It's made of plastic. Blue rope doesn't go away.", answered Alfie. Freya looked around the beach and found a large stone. She had to lift it with both hands before she threw it into the river. The stone fell short of the rope. "I want it to go away. I want it to fucking go away!", Freya shouted into the swirling water. Alfie started picking up stones and throwing them at the rope. "The fish will probably eat it, Freya.", he said, "Then it will be all gone away forever.". "You've made a mess of everything.", said Freya. Alfie turned around, pointed at the tree, and replied, "You said you liked my LOVES.". Freya followed his finger and nodded her approval. Then she said, "Come on. Let's go home.".

As they made their way towards Dunkeld Alfie asked Freya what her favourite games were and told her the names of his favourite streamers. Freya pointed out the carvings she could see on other trees and Alfie agreed with her that using a cross instead of carving the word AND was cheating. When they came to the stone steps that led up to the bridge that crossed the Tay Freya let Alfie walk ahead of her in case he fell backwards. By the time they were halfway across the bridge Freya could see that the fish bar was open and she pulled a crumpled ten pound note from her pocket. "Do you want some chips, Alfie?", she asked. Alfie smiled at her and replied, "Yes, please!". "What about some chocolate juice?", Freya joked. "They won't have any. They don't know that I've invented it yet.", said Alfie. "Oh, yes. I forgot about that. I'll keep it a secret until you're older then.", Freya whispered. They came to a stop at the junction on the Dunkeld side of the bridge. The traffic was busy. Freya took Alfie's hand. It felt warmer than hers. A Land Rover came to a stop and the driver waved them onto the road. They crossed over safely.

10. THE LIGHT

Brendan Shaw peeled his left cheek from a sodden pillow, rolled his sagging body across his bed, then felt for the floor with his right foot before deciding that he'd need to open an eye. His cheap watch informed him that it was almost midday, but he knew that an expensive one wouldn't have been any kinder to him. Brendan hated waking up. His days were usually filled with an unpredictable mixture of pain and boredom. So, his inbuilt hunting and gathering instincts had, for the past decade or so, been focused on searching for enough pills and alcohol to consume each day to ensure that his body was as numb as his mind was by the time he lay his head down again at night. Sleep never came quickly to Brendan but, when it eventually arrived, he always hoped that it would be his last.

He got to his feet then stumbled towards the bathroom, pausing on the landing to collect a fresh towel. Brendan was careful not to look in the mirror, in case someone who looked like his late Father would gaze back at him.

The shower always seemed to clean away more than just sweat and, for a few minutes at least, as Brendan dried himself and got dressed he felt much the same as he had done in his youth. One of the few things that made him happy these days was the sensation of wearing a brand new pair of socks. They could be any colour, other than white. As far as Brendan was concerned, only women could make white socks look good. Today he opted for a new pair of orange socks. They were made of a thin material, and they felt good inside his dark grey suede trainers. These little flashes of colour were mostly hidden under a heavy pair of dark green corduroy trousers, which were held up by a brown leather belt. A navy sweater, a black waterproof jacket and a dark grey flat cap completed his outfit.

Brendan filled his jacket pockets with his phone, house keys, wallet, a handful of painkillers and a packet of mints. Then he stuffed yesterday's loose change into the right hand pocket of his corduroys, before feeling the stubble on his face. He was certain that it still looked as grey as it was the last time he had caught sight of it.

The Bowler's Arms was a ten minute walk from Brendan's house and, often, a twenty-three minute stumble back again through the streets of Belfast. Today the sky hung grey and low, hiding the city from the rest of the World. The air felt heavy and the traffic hummed as Brendan made his way towards the pub. He could hear the hammering and drilling of a building site somewhere out of view. As Brendan passed the entrance to the local supermarket an elderly gentleman nodded at him and, without thinking about it, Brendan gave him The Light.

The Light was the only thing that kept Brendan going. He had only become aware of it recently. The morning after he had contemplated doing away with himself, to be precise. Since then he had noticed his ability to gift other people with The Light. He had to be careful with it though. If he gave it away to the wrong people he ended up feeling more ill than usual. He had convinced himself that The Light was something to do with the power to live. Brendan felt he could now give away part of what was left of his life to others. He could recharge them.

When he pushed open the door of the pub he could smell stale cigarette smoke, even though no one had been allowed to smoke inside the building for well over a decade. Brendan noticed that Michael was behind the bar, and that suited him. Michael dressed in a style that made him look like an undertaker at the end of a particularly taxing day. Brendan liked that he could simply ask for a lager, rather than a brand of beer, and that's what he did. This was met with a cough from Michael, before he busied himself with the order. Brendan gazed at the television set, which was high up in the corner of the room, until his pint was ready. He then handed Michael a ten pound note and waited for his change. The pub was mainly populated by men whose facial expressions suggested their dog had died the night before. An elderly couple sat next to the window, drinking in silence. Brendan responded to a cough behind him and pocketed his change before lifting his pint to his face and gulping hard. He couldn't work out where a smell of eggs was coming from, but he hoped the aroma wasn't coming off the lager.

Brendan took a couple of painkillers out of his pocket, put them in his mouth, and washed them down with another gulp of lager. The smell of eggs was everywhere now which wasn't great, but it meant it was either coming from the kitchen or one of the old boys. There was no way that the stench was coming from what was left of Brendan's lager. Although, he downed the rest of it, just in case. He placed another ten pound note on the bar and asked Michael for "A couple of pints of stout for the corner.", before nodding at an empty table with his head and making his way to the toilet.

By the time Brendan had returned to the bar two creamy pints of stout were waiting for him at his corner table, along with an unfamiliar woman with a suitcase who was busy plugging her phone into the wall. "Hi, sorry, the guy said I could charge my phone here. Hope you don't mind?". Brendan sat down beside her, shrugged his shoulders, and said, "Aye, work away.". He liked her scent, it was a vast improvement on stale smoke and eggs. "Is that an English accent?", he asked. "I grew up in Manchester. I live here now though. Are you thirsty?".

Brendan looked down at the table and, for a moment, felt embarrassed by the pair of pints. "Saves me getting up again.", he said as he lifted the one that was nearest to her up to his mouth. He sipped at the pint, leaving himself with a little creamy moustache. "I was only joking. Look, that's mine coming now.". Michael was making his way over to the table holding a pint of lager. "There you go love. Is that charging alright for you?". Brendan noticed that Michael's cough had cleared up, and the smell of eggs was back. "Yes, thank you very much.", she said. As Michael made his way back to the bar Brendan asked her what her name was. "Jodie.". Her eyes were large and bright, her cheeks glowed and her white teeth dazzled. Brendan decided that he quite fancied her, then warned her about the lager. "I'm Brendan. Here, you can have my other stout if you want. That lager is off.". "How can you tell?", she asked. "Well, it smells funny.", said Brendan. Although, the smell of eggs seemed to have lifted. "Actually, I think you're alright. It must be that barman.". Brendan gazed at Michael, who coughed then looked away.

"What's with the suitcase?", Brendan asked. "I'm just back from visiting my sister, Laura, in Glasgow. It was nice to see her, but it rained the whole time.". While Jodie spoke Brendan sipped at his stout and his eyes drank her in. She spoke with her hands, like she was conducting an invisible orchestra. Brendan liked the way she dressed. Her orange jumper reminded him of his socks. Dark blue jeans hugged her thighs and her socks were black with little white stars, or falling snow. "I like your trainers.", he said, as he stretched his back and adjusted his neck. Jodie looked down at her feet and lifted her toes. "I've got two pairs of them. These grey ones and a red pair.".

The door of the pub opened, but it wasn't anyone Brendan knew. Just another old boy, soaked through. "I see you've brought the weather with you.", he said, smiling at Jodie. "Don't say that! I'm actually very good with the weather. If I want it to be sunny I can make it happen.". "Oh aye?!", Brendan raised his left eyebrow and took a proper gulp of his stout. "I'm telling you! I just think happy thoughts and the sun comes out.".

There was something about Jodie that made Brendan relax. He really did like her smell, and it wasn't even perfume. She started talking about architecture, and he couldn't really keep up with her. She was very bright. Brendan couldn't work out if it was the stout beginning to work, or if Michael had turned the heating up, but he was roasting. He unzipped his jacket and took it off whilst Jodie talked about some new building in the Titanic Quarter. He wanted to take his cap off, but was embarrassed about his balding head. The heat got the better of him though and he took it off. He even mopped his brow with it before tossing it on top of his jacket. "It's boiling in here now. Are you warm, or is it just me?". Brendan stretched his back again. "I told you, if I'm thinking happy thoughts the sun comes out!", Jodie giggled and her eyes and teeth dazzled Brendan again. "Are you trying to tell me it's sunny inside now? You're making this up as you go along.". Brendan looked up at the television and sipped at his pint. "Keep an eye on my things, will you? I'm just going to the loo.", said Jodie. Brendan nodded at the television screen.

Michael made his way over to the table while Brendan necked the last of his first stout. "Same again lad?". "Aye, a lager and a... Actually, make it two lagers.". Michael headed off to the bar with the empty pint glass as Brendan searched through his jacket pockets for money, another couple of painkillers and a mint. He swallowed the pills with a healthy gulp of stout and then began sucking the mint. The flavour combination left a lot to be desired. Brendan was gazing at the television again by the time Michael returned to the table and set the fresh pints down. Brendan handed over another tenner, "If there's any change you can keep it.". Michael nodded and made his way back towards the bar, collecting the odd glass as he went.

"You didn't run off then?". Jodie returned to her seat and checked her phone. "Aye, I thought about it. Here, I bought you another pint.", Brendan pointed at the drink, as if she wouldn't have known where it was. "That was very nice of you. I've a message from Laura here asking if I've arrived safely.". "Ask her if the sun has come out in Glasgow, will you?", Brendan grinned.

Jodie typed a message into her phone as Brendan stretched out his legs and looked around the room. He wasn't sure if The Bowler's Arms had ever seen better days. As pubs go, it was grim. The low lighting made a feature out of the television. Everyone seemed to look at it, but nobody ever watched it. Jodie set her phone down beside her. It was still connected to the wall. They both lifted their drinks in unison then looked at each other. "Cheers?", inquired Jodie. "Cheers.", replied Brendan, and they chinked their glasses together then drank from them at the same time. Jodie joined Brendan in looking around the room, before she turned to him and said, "Your eyes are stupendous.". Brendan smiled at her. He didn't know that eyes could be stupendous. Maybe that's what her eyes were too? He wasn't too sure though, and thought he might embarrass himself. "I think your eyes are lovely. I think you're lovely, actually.", Brendan said, hoping that it sounded alright. Jodie smiled and Brendan felt really warm inside. He hadn't felt like that in years. Jodie took his hand and said, "The best place to see The Light is in the dark.".

ii. POSTFACE

I'm writing these words in early December, 2022. I had hoped this book would have been ready to publish last month. However, a few weeks back I was tasked with writing 1,000 words for 70, a book to be published by Bill Drummond's Penkiln Burn imprint in late April, 2023. The book will be a biography celebrating seven decades of Bill and it will be released on his birthday. He asked me to write about his life when he was 31 years of age. I sent him my chapter late last night and he got back to me early this morning. Bill thanked me for more than rising to the challenge and told me my work was brilliant in all sorts of ways. He also invited me along to a gig with Hollie McNish and Michael Pedersen in Edinburgh on the night before his birthday. I will be helping Bill in Belfast further down the line and I view that almost like a graduation. It was reading Bill's story, Making Soup, 20 years ago that made me realise that Art in Belfast could be more than three letters painted on a gable end wall. Bill has taught me many things about Art since then.

I was recently diagnosed with Obsessive Compulsive Disorder. Bill told me that all great front men have OCD, "It goes with the territory.". Along with helping me deal with The Real World as a creative person, Bill has also educated me a little about nature, specifically weeds. Whenever I turned 41 Bill informed me that I share the same birthday as his sister, Jane, and that I should look out for Michaelmas Daisies around that time of year. So, this year, 2022, whenever I turned 42, I found lots of them growing in my own garden. Once located, I looked up a video on how best to dry flowers, picked myself a bunch of those birthday daisies and hung them upside down to dry out next to one of Bill's posters from 2019. The sun was setting by the time I stood back and began to admire the drying flowers. I thought they looked beautiful, but I also knew that they were upside down and dead. I decided to take a photograph of those daisies next to Bill's poster as I felt they summed up the journey I had been on from before the Coronavirus pandemic until the moment I pressed the shutter. It is the image I will use on the front cover of this book.

Nina Kraviz is a fellow Libran, and we are also in the habit of wishing each other happy birthdays. I love Nina, she's the most vibrant person I know. Quite the opposite of me, as I'm a fairly quiet person, an observer. Nina, instead, throws herself into life. I'm often amazed at how her mind works. I've had conversations with Nina that dance between subjects like writing, languages, psychology, art, fashion, design, travel and, of course, music. I suppose it's the perfect brain for a talented DJ to have. Inquisitive, opinionated, deep and very funny. I was with Nina in Belfast in late February of this year, just as our phones informed us of what Wikipedia now calls the 2022 Russian invasion of Ukraine. Nina posted a message calling for peace on Instagram. However, the post drew in a lot of angry comments and personal insults. It reminded me of growing up during The Troubles in Northern Ireland and visiting my family in England at times when people from my country were bombing places like London and Manchester. I wasn't personally responsible for any of that stuff, but I was subjected to anti-Irish insults nonetheless.

I did my best to support Nina. She was in Belfast to headline a night at my favourite club, Shine. I told her that she'd be fine in the city as the people there had been through conflict and peace, and now they just wanted to live happier lives. In truth, I don't think the Belfast I grew up in really exists any more, and the majority of the people dancing at Shine that night were likely to have been born after the Good Friday Agreement was signed. However, Belfast did not let me down and the atmosphere inside the club was fantastic. It was wonderful to watch young people dancing together after a couple of years of lockdowns and quarantines. Whenever we got backstage after the show I handed Nina a copy of my book, No Rest For The Listener. She asked me if it was signed, and it was. It makes me smile knowing that both Bill and Nina have asked me for signed copies of my books. They are my favourite artists and without them I'm not sure if the books I've written would exist. I also find them quite similar in the way they think about Art. Nina's 2019 Coachella performance was just as self-destructive as Bill's at the 1992 Brit Awards.

So far, this Postface has mostly been an exercise in fame by association. That's something I have learned from Bill. Other ways that he suggests artists can find fame is by creating work that is about, or comments upon, either fame, violence, sex or death. I have done my best to fill the pages of this book with tales that cover one, or more, of those subjects. One of the nice things I find about reaching middle age is the sense of overview I now have with the projects I work on. I am also enjoying becoming comfortable with who I am. In the modern age this seems to involve applying labels like Asexual and Obsessive Compulsive Disorder to how I describe myself. These descriptors help to open up my World to like-minded folk. Recently, the Irish writer, musician and podcaster, Blindboy Boatclub congratulated me on all I had achieved while having OCD. I just wish I'd applied those labels earlier in life, as I may have had to suffer a little less over the years. Although, perhaps, the stories I tell wouldn't be as rich had that been the case? I do feel for everyone who's labels aren't as easily accepted by others as my own are. I hope that changes.

Bill Drummond's warning to me upon turning 40 that it would be one of the more difficult years of my life certainly proved to be one worth taking notice of. I have spent much of these past couple of years feeling depressed and thinking about death. I can remember in the early stages of the pandemic reading that there was little Art that made reference to the 1918 Flu Pandemic. So, I decided that I would make plenty of notes about the World as it was while I wrote this book. After reading Covid Shebeen, Scaramanga Silk told me he felt it featured too many references to the rules of lockdown, but I kept them all in. I'm glad that I did because, even from this short distance, much of it seems bizarre. I actually got the idea for writing that story from tales my Grandfather told me about illegal drinking dens in Belfast during the first decade of The Troubles. As I watched early news reports from Ireland in lockdown I found myself thinking that there would likely be similar shebeens operating then. I was right. Before long, several illegal drinking dens had been raided in Laois, Meath and Westmeath in the Republic Of Ireland.

I will now slip effortlessly into detailing the methods I used whilst crafting the tales contained in this book. I am able to do this as I have already written several nonfiction books, the most recent of which took me just 12 weeks to write and became a number 1 bestseller. So, I can now write nonfiction as easily as I can talk. Unfortunately, this was not the case whenever it came to me writing fiction. These stories, with the exception of Ben Smyth, each took me a long time to write.

The tale that hung over the entire process of writing this book was Lights Out In The Booth. I got the idea for writing a story about vampire DJ's the first time I met Nina. It was shortly after 3am in Belfast and Nina was about to travel to Germany to DJ later that morning, and from there onto Paris to headline a festival at night before she could finally sleep. She doesn't take drugs, and she had just handed me the full bottle of champagne that was on her rider. So, I asked her how she was able to work like that. She told me that the energy from the crowd lifted her enough to keep going. So, in my mind, I thought of her as an energy vampire.

I told my Irish cousin, Kate, about my plans to write a short story about vampire DJ's and she was really excited to read it. Although, she felt disappointed with the finished tale because it ended before the vampires went to the club. She then wrote her own version of what she hoped would happen once my characters went to the Rave. I told her that I felt her version of the story would likely be very close to the narrative most readers could conjure up in their heads after reading my effort. Therefore, I had come to the conclusion that I didn't need to actually write that part of the story at all. Kate then had a bit of a lightbulb moment and found it quite amusing that she had filled in the same blanks as other readers were likely to upon reading my short story. I had learned about the art of giving people just enough of the picture that they could complete the rest of it themselves through reading short stories by James Kelman, Laura Hird and Bernard MacLaverty. Many of James Kelman's earliest stories are very short indeed, some only a paragraph long. Although, they each contain enough detail to keep the tale going in the mind of the reader.

I knew that I didn't have the skills to write my vampire story whenever I set out to write this book. The first fictional story I wrote, The Light, felt pretty close to writing about my own life at that time, albeit sprinkled with a little magical thinking. I used very simple tricks like writing for all the senses. The tale has the classic three act structure of set up, conflict and resolution. The most important thing that I learned about ending a short story is to leave the reader with the feeling that the narrative breaks off but life goes on for the characters in the tale. It was also useful to discover through writing this book that people don't want to read about me they want to read about themselves. So, I would add lots of very specific details about items in my stories, but I did my best not to do that too much with the characters. I felt that by leaving how the people in my little epics looked fairly vague then readers were more likely to see themselves, or someone they knew, in their mirrors. Each of the stories attempts to deal with a universal theme. Usually the lead character is contemplating the human condition. So, that makes them relatable.

The biggest discovery for me as a writer was how the point of view I chose to write each story in could completely change how the reader would experience it. I've read Philip Pullman writing about point of view and describing it as deciding where to put the camera that the reader will be looking through. The Light is written in third person. So, the reader gets a big overview of everything that is going on inside the World of that story with a narrator guiding them through the tale. The third person point of view is the most popular in publishing and my book is no exception. Six of the ten tales are told that way; Death Notes, Fear Of Falling, Covid Shebeen, How I Got My Scar, Freya Loves Grace and The Light. In first person the reader is told the story by the lead character. The Comedown and Ben Smyth are both written that way. This leaves us with just the two strangest stories in the book remaining. The Plant Room is written in second person singular, with the reader placed inside the mind of the lead character. Finally, Lights Out In The Booth is written in first person plural, with a pair of lead characters telling the tale in unison.

I wrote lots of notes about each of the stories in advance of them being written. I found that if I left the stories to develop over a long time in my head some of them would begin to mingle with each other. This often led to a couple of story ideas becoming a single tale that was stronger than either of the original ideas on their own. I have never written a second draft of anything in my life, but I am very particular about how each page looks. Presumably, this is related to my OCD. I like to leave no blank space on my pages, including this one. I was approached by a literary agent towards the end of writing this book. They look after a lot of successful writers and seemed interested in what I do. However, I couldn't imagine creating anything with any sort of middle man in mind, ever. Just as I'm glad I decided to decline the advances of a major record company in my twenties, I'm happy that I decided to continue to do my own thing in my forties. I chatted to Bill about it and he said he has been involved with several publishers over the years and none of those relationships proved to be satisfactory. They wanted more than he wished to give.

I was very stressed at times during the writing of this book, both through dealing with the lives of the characters on my pages and getting on with my own life in The Real World. On one visit to see my family in Belfast I decided to leave within hours of arrival as I couldn't handle being out of my routine, and I found other people very draining to be around. I've always had difficulty hanging out with others, particularly at parties, on birthdays and at Christmas time. I can manage for an hour or so, then I tend to go off to a room on my own. I recently listened to an episode of the Adam Buxton Podcast in which Adam was talking to Fran Healy, the lead singer of Travis. Fran was chatting about being at a party at Billy Connolly's house in Scotland. It sounded like quite a celebrity bash and it seemed to go on for several days. Fran said he quickly found a quiet room in the house and went there every day by himself to just be alone. One afternoon the door to the room opened and Billy walked in. "What the fuck are you doing here?", Billy asked. When Fran told him, Billy confessed that he too had had enough and wanted to be alone.

Being a DJ in my twenties meant that I had to be a very social person at times. So, in order to mask the fact that I'm deeply introverted, I would get drunk or high. Now that I live in chronic pain I have to take a lot of prescription drugs. So, I don't take any other drugs, and I very rarely drink alcohol now. Nina has even noticed this. One of her Belfast gigs for Shine was outdoors in front of 5,000 people in Custom House Square. I was dancing about on the stage and Nina offered me a glass of her champagne, but I declined. That's not something I would have done when I was younger, but I'm more comfortable being me now. The closer I get to being myself the more people seem to be drawn to me. Whenever I think about that I conclude that anyone who I think of as cool tends to be very comfortable just being themselves. It seems to have little to do with how a person looks, what they wear or the music they're into. Cool might simply relate to acceptance of oneself. If so, I guess I now have that in my favour. Humans seem to spend a lot of their time creating elaborate masks to wear in public. That could very well be a waste of time.

Ben Smyth was written very quickly in a successful attempt to break through creative block between writing How I Got My Scar and The Plant Room. I'm very happy with that story. I like that there is so much going on in Ben's World that he is too young to grasp. Yet, at the same time, his simple way of viewing the World has a real humour and beauty to it. I also enjoyed writing about children in Freya Loves Grace, although it deals with darker themes. In fact, many of my tales are quite dark in nature but, hopefully, I deliver them in a way that isn't too bleak. Laura Hird's stories can be exceptionally dark, and I wouldn't usually be drawn to art that is so grim. However, I can tell that she is a supremely gifted storyteller. I feel quite safe being led wherever her words take me. I was chatting with Blindboy about Laura's collection, Nail And Other Stories, as someone in the audience at one of his live podcasts had thrown it onstage. I like how great stories find their way to the right people, eventually. James Kelman's stories can also be grim, but he's so gifted at being able to make his readers care for even the worst of his characters.

What I found when reading the short story collections of Bernard MacLaverty was that I didn't connect with them all, but the ones that I enjoyed lived on in my mind for a long time after I'd put his books down. The stories in my own collection are quite diverse. So, I don't expect that many people will like all of them. However, I do hope that most readers will enjoy several of the tales enough that they wish they were longer. That's a nice feeling.
I wanted to push myself beyond my comfort zone, particularly when writing about sex. It's a challenge to put that stuff on paper and make it seem real and relatable. Kate Bosworth, the very talented host of the seminal underground electronic music show Dark Train, contacted me after reading the asexual sex scene in The Comedown. She loved how the paragraph about the blow job was so matter of fact and said she found herself screaming, "Give her what she wants!". It was great to get that sort of feedback as often the more explicit stories were met with silence. My Mum let me know that she really enjoyed How I Got My Scar though, which was great, as it was a difficult story to write.

In order to get Death Notes right I read several collections of short stories written by women and I made notes about the things that made the tales different from the way I was writing. The main thing I noticed was that a lot of the stories I read that were written by women included characters that weren't essential to the plot, but added colour to the World they were writing about. There might be a drunken discussion with a taxi driver, a polite conversation with a gardener or even a bit of internal dialogue that didn't seem to go anywhere. I hope what I'm writing now hasn't got you shouting at the page. I'm simply reporting my discoveries! Anyway, when I wrote Death Notes I added a lot of detail about the neighbour of the main character. None of that stuff really needed to be in the story, but it did make it read like the other stories I had been studying. I knew that what I'd done had worked the day after I had uploaded it for my test audience to read. There was a lot of great feedback from women and my Mum text me to say that she had read it to my Grandmother, who is now in her 80's, and both of them had really enjoyed the story.

Fear Of Falling was my attempt to look at life through the eyes of someone like my Nanny. The opening section took a long time to write as I felt the pace should match the speed, or lack thereof, of someone in their later years. I enjoy writing nonfiction as it's simply a matter of writing down my thoughts. These Postface pages are rattling out of my mind and through my fingers with ease. What I discovered writing fiction is that it involves a lot of waiting around for the subconscious to deliver the goods. That seems to be why a lot of fiction writers get their work done early in the morning while their brains are still in that slightly out of focus, dreamlike, almost high, state. Barry The Tank Taylor was a fully formed character who appeared in my mind just when I needed him, midway through Fear Of Falling. As soon as Barry showed up everything fitted into place and the end of the story was just a matter of mirroring the opening section. The tale proved to be another hit with my Mum and Grandmother. Not long after that I felt that I had gathered all of the writing tools I would need to create my vampire story, Lights Out In The Booth.

Once I had written all ten of the short stories in this book I decided to shuffle the deck in order to open with The Comedown. However, if you have an obsessive mind like mine, you may be interested to know the original sequence the tales were written in. I wrote The Light first, followed by Covid Shebeen, Freya Loves Grace, Death Notes, How I Got My Scar and Ben Smyth. After that came The Plant Room, Fear Of Falling and The Comedown. The final story I wrote was Lights Out In The Booth. I did have some notes for further stories, but after I had written ten I was exhausted and I felt I had given all I could and made the book as good as I possibly could. I did my best to write characters of different ages, boys and girls, men and women. I tried writing from unusual points of view too. Scaramanga Silk suggested I read a book called The Notebook by Agota Kristof. I have since recommended it to Bill Drummond. The book is about twins surviving the Second World War. It's a dark tale delivered from a strange point of view, first person plural. I found the style so unsettling that I decided to use it for Lights Out In The Booth.

It feels strange bringing this book to a close as I have lived with it for years, both on my desktop and in my mind. Once it is published, early in 2023 I hope, I will turn The Comedown into an audio play, using the songs that I mention in the story along with sound effects and my own voice reading the tale. I'm not an actor. So, Richard and Tina will share the same voice, my voice. It's a voice that many people seem to like though. My process during the writing of this book of uploading short video readings has really helped me to just press Record and get the job done. I would like the year ahead to be one in which I focus on creating audio content, like podcasts, DJ mixes and new music. I might even record audio books of my work to date if the mood takes me. Right now the idea of writing another book is not something that appeals to me. The part of my brain that deals with sequencing words feels close to burnout. However, in the years ahead I hope to work with both Bill and Nina and I'm sure that will lead to me having more stories to tell. Perhaps, further down the line, I might even feel the urge to write some fiction again.

If you have enjoyed this book you can help me out by writing positive reviews online in places like Amazon and Goodreads. Marketing genius Seth Godin suggests that I may only require ten people who REALLY like my work to amplify my message. Perhaps you could be one of those ten people? If so, then tell ten of your friends about this book and, hopefully, each of those people will tell ten more people about The Comedown and before long, well, I don't know really. World domination?

If you would like to stay up to date with what I do then you should follow me on places like Twitter, Instagram and Bandcamp. If you are reading this book many years in the future then that might be as relevant as asking you to follow me on MySpace or to ring my house phone. If search engines still exist then look me up. If I am no longer alive then maybe you could sort out a Wikipedia page for me, or perhaps you could make a documentary about my life and work? Whatever you decide to do I would like you to know that I love you, that I think you matter and that you have great taste. So, Keep Dreaming! Yours, Stephen Clarke 1980.

iii. AFTERWORD BY SCARAMANGA SILK

The Inkling Instinct

6 gigabytes. That was the moment.

As I sit here composing the words to close this book, I am reflecting upon how we have arrived at this point. In recent years, my journey as a DJ and Music Producer has taken some unexpected turns. From having Snooker legend Steve Davis rate my album, Designer Scribble, as one of his Best Of 2016, to Discogs announcing in 2021 that a copy of my 2008 single, Choose Your Weapon, had become the Most Expensive Record Ever Sold on their platform, at £30,000, it has been quite a ride! However, amongst all the music, I have also been focusing on a literary path, wrestling the written word in a bid to complete my own book. While I have ventured into this new chapter, being able to liaise, discuss, and watch another musician tread the same trail has been both invaluable and inspiring. I also appear to have influenced his progress to the page too...

Let's rewind the record to 2017 when I was fortunate enough to attend Welcome To The Dark Ages, an event held by Bill Drummond and Jimmy Cauty under their Justified Ancients of Mu Mu moniker. Having grown up on their music as The KLF (and in other guises), I had become aware of the mythology surrounding these rather alternative pop icons. As well as topping the charts and rocking dance floors, the duo had written a book on how to have a Number One hit single, created an award for Worst Artist Of The Year, and burned a million quid! So, when the chance to be one of only 400 participants at their new happening arose, I felt it was essential to be present.

Nobody knew quite what to expect during those August days in Liverpool. Furthermore, it had been announced that no press would be allowed inside the proceedings. As a keen student of Bill and Jimmy's work I felt it important to document whatever was going to occur. Given their track record, this was likely to be an historical occasion for the art world. The website https://www.welcometothedarkages.com/ was born.

Initially, my plan was to blog a round-up of each of the five days in real time. However, the project turned into two years of reporting as it grew to become a community hub with contributions from the audience and members of the team involved in hosting affairs. Although, there was one main exception...

Inevitably, certain aspects of the event did make the headlines. This was mainly due to the publication of their new novel, 2023, also hitting stores at the same time. Radical bookshop, News From Nowhere, had a midnight opening with Bill and Jimmy arriving in their famous Ice Cream Van. Hundreds of fans queued in anticipation and the media relayed the story across breakfast news the following morning. Over the days that followed, as I scrolled through Twitter, I wanted to see how the outside world was interpreting what was happening here. In Scotland, someone began to catch my eye with his passionate fandom and exquisite knowledge of the artists. He was watching matters closely and was clearly consuming as much information as he could. Then he published the tweet that convinced me to contact him.

I would love to share the exact wording, but this guy deletes the majority of his online footprint as he values digital scarcity. In the post, he divulged how he had downloaded 6 gigabytes of content about Welcome To The Dark Ages from news coverage and social media. This was the perfect person. This was the kind of mind and personality that my website needed next. This was the most dedicated of people. If anybody could give a great perspective of the event as an outsider looking in, it was him. This individual was Stephen Clarke 1980. Before I asked Clarke to contribute to the website, I was not aware that he was in the midst of becoming an author or had any previous writing experience of this nature. Initially, I knew that, like myself, he was a DJ and also a music producer. However, after making my request, I was informed that he was halfway through penning his autobiography! This boded well. To my surprise, only 48 hours later, I was in receipt of an 8000-word story. Nobody had written to that length for the website previously. This was not just a case of quantity. The quality was high too. Really high.

Entitled Liberation Loophole (A reference to an as yet unused KLF pseudonym), this blog post was unlike any other. Our narrator took us on a journey from boyhood discovery to epic musical fantasy by weaving autobiographical anecdotes with exaggerated euphoria about the events. His words were sewn together with wisdom, wit, knowledge and, above all, an unrivalled passion. Character and life poured from the screen. I had to get this guy's number immediately in order to pay my respects to his skills. Penmanship of this calibre needed to be acknowledged, and it was. Clarke's essay became the most read article on the website. Not bad for someone who hadn't been asked to write anything since High School!

Picking up the needle and skipping forward.. November 2017 ushered in the promised autobiography, Deleted Scenes. I was intrigued, as the vast majority of books in this category are from people off the telly, troubled Pop icons, and glamorous A-List stars. It was so refreshing to see someone from a World I shared tell the story of their life's travels. His was a voice I could relate to.

Across the pages we learned of his time growing up in Belfast during The Troubles, his highs and lows in love, and his nights spinning Techno behind the decks. Each new page showed a man who was prepared to be open, honest, bold, and vulnerable. The joy of this writing is found in the author's ability to spin any yarn in an engaging and entertaining fashion. I have no doubt that his Irish heritage is a factor in this gift.

Flipping the wax and dropping the stylus, we head into 2018 and 2019.. In these years two further books were released. Keep Dreaming: A Guide To Real Life skilfully blended personal tales with advice for pretty much any area of human existence. No Rest For The Listener carried on from his previous titles whilst focusing on observations about music and the arts to join dots that had previously been unseen.

Pausing the sounds for a moment.. Let's gaze into another sphere. Not only had Clarke been hammering out a book a year, many of his studio productions had also been surfacing during that time, covering melancholic Ambient to crunching industrial Techno.

As his releases hit the internet they were regularly finding a place in my own DJ sets. Alas, our artist does not put his music out into the world in a conventional fashion. Much like his social media posts, finding a Stephen Clarke 1980 album is almost impossible just a few months after it has graced Bandcamp, as it will have been deleted. If you were not there in the moment, then that moment did not hang around to wait for you. All of his future profits and additional exposure will have been forfeited. New projects await and they cannot be created with a pen in the past or a needle on nostalgia.

Hitting play again, resuming the crackle and bass.. We are back in 2022. By this time, Clarke and I have conversed on many occasions about all kinds of aspects of life as a creative person. It has become clear to me that he lives by his own rules, has a distinct vision of how he wants his art to be formed, and is not one for compromise. For me, these qualities define a real artist. Even his tweets are unique in their wording, formatting, and message. No characters are wasted and no statements are throwaways.

As The Comedown And Other Stories is in development, Clarke embarks on short daily video tweets with updates on his process and progress as well as prose previews to entice his followers. This look behind the curtain at a writer at work in real time is invaluable. The insight, the challenges, the research, the small wins, the lessons learned, the synapses firing, the connections being made – all are on show as we drive towards the final full stop. Along the way, some of his writing appears on a blog, for a limited time only of course. It delights. We witness an author at play. Stories from different voices, times, and ages are presented. From a little boy observing his day to vampire DJ's living in Hell, we encounter an imagination in action with flair and flamboyance.

Much like the rotating vinyl records that have scored Clarke's adventures, his writing has come full circle too. I could not have imagined that from a single blog post four books would then follow. Having enjoyed his first three autobiographical publications, I contacted Stephen to propose that it might be good idea for him to try to develop a fictional work during the pandemic years.

His first piece back in 2017, Liberation Loophole, had sewn the seeds with its alternative account of Welcome To The Dark Ages in a warped and funky version of The KLF universe. I was convinced that he could create his own cast of characters on their own stage and that it would likely be well received as he appeared to have a natural knack for such a style of writing. Surprisingly, this notion had not already presented itself to his consciousness. Thankfully, the injected idea was soon cemented and came to complete fruition. To now see The Comedown And Other Stories solely focus on the imagination of this author is a real treat and joy.

Small signals have power. A tweet about downloading online coverage and social media content showed me an individual who cares about detail and who is dedicated to a cause. It wasn't much to go on but my instincts proved to be correct and we have been rewarded by the artist's continued body of work. Smatterings of fiction within a blog post about a real world event demonstrated an ability to tell stories beyond the autobiographical. A nudge in that direction has resulted in this very book.

An inkling, when followed fully, can produce wonderful results. I'm so appreciative that Clarke was open to some simple suggestions and formulated them into his own sublime art. In turn, his journey has invigorated my own move into the literary World and for that I am also grateful.

Who knows what direction Stephen Clarke 1980 will take next. He may serve up some banging new music. More literature may grace our shelves too. Perhaps he may even focus his writing on the wit that so many readers have noticed in his books. No matter what path is taken, we can be assured that it will be done on his own terms and in his own unique way. This is what we need.

Scaramanga Silk
29.09.2022
London

http://scaramangasi.lk/
https://www.facebook.com/scaramangasilk
https://twitter.com/scaramanga_silk

iv. ACKNOWLEDGEMENTS

I'd like to thank my family for reading each of these stories as they were written, before providing me with either words of encouragement or complete silence depending upon the sexual content of each tale. To my Grandmother, Mary, who enjoyed the segments which were deemed suitable to be read aloud to her. To my Mum, who read every word and liked them all. My younger Brother, Paul, and my Aunt, Michelle, were more selective, but knew my genius frolicked along each and every line of text regardless of their gaze. To my Cousin, Jack, for dancing with Nina Kraviz, and his Dad, my Uncle, Paul, who reckons Bill Drummond knows more about life than most. To Kate Costello for sharing her vast knowledge of vampires with me across multiple voice messages. To Scaramanga Silk, without whom this book would likely not exist. To Kate Bosworth and Grant McPhee for providing me with wonderful quotes to grace its cover. To my pals Budgie, Stu and Zippy for having interesting names and providing banter and memes.

To Conor Garrett for recording the moment I fixed a microphone lead that Jimmy Cauty had kicked out and broadcasting it on the BBC. To Gimpo, Rachel Barker, Tommy Calderbank, Lisa Lovebucket, Lou Lou Whalley and everyone who made my trip to Liverpool to DJ for The JAMs such a wonderful experience. To Phil Kieran and Anthony Ferris for their good patter and hospitality at Shine, Belfast. To Andrew Shaw, Alan Dunn, Salena Godden, Blindboy Boatclub, Tommie Sunshine and every creative person in my social circle who fuelled my fire on a regular basis throughout the years it took me to write this book. To my Italian friends Morris Antonello and Sabrina Chiesurin for their optimism and belief that I should contemplate doing a book signing in a local shop, even after I assured them that they would be the only punters there. Finally, to you, dear reader, for making it this far. If you were searching for your own name here and I have failed to deliver the goods I can only apologise. You can, perhaps, take comfort from the fact that I have, once again, left you with that special feeling of wanting more. Keep dreaming, Stephen Clarke 1980.

Printed in Great Britain
by Amazon